"I've been w... Nicholas."

There was a seductive undertone to Casi's soft voice, and when Nicholas greeted her with a kiss her response went far beyond a casual salutation.

She raised her hands to the back of his head, running her fingers through his thick, wavy hair. Then gorging herself on the feel of his skin, she touched him as she had longed to touch him for days and days....

Nicholas gently, slowly, lifted his mouth from hers. "Casi?" he whispered huskily. "Remember what you once said about there being a time and a place? I've just thought of the ideal place."

A stab of exquisite anticipation left Casi breathless. "Good...but what about the time?"

Swinging her into his arms, Nicholas murmured, "It's about 10:45. Will that do?"

"Perfect," she breathed in his ear. "I've always said 10:45 is the best time of day to make love...."

THE AUTHOR

What with the booming shellcraft business she and husband Dick share, her career as a writer and her five terrific children, Jane Edwards has everything she's ever wanted. She describes herself as a gloriously happy woman who believes one hundred percent in love, marriage and lasting romance.

Listen with Your Heart is Jane's first Harlequin Temptation—and the beginning of yet another personal success story. Her impressive publishing background includes several mystery-romance novels, a variety of nonfiction assignments and more than forty short stories and novelettes.

Listen with Your Heart

JANE EDWARDS

Harlequin Books

TORONTO • NEW YORK • LONDON
AMSTERDAM • PARIS • SYDNEY • HAMBURG
STOCKHOLM • ATHENS • TOKYO • MILAN

For a very special group of art-show friends:
Watercolorist Phyllis Humphrey
Promoter Judy Cunningham
Enamelist Gerry Raddatz and her sister, Ruthie,
and
Artist Lenore Masterson

Published January 1986

ISBN 0-373-25190-4

1

I DON'T LIKE HIM, Casi thought, understating the depth of her feelings considerably.

Her long tapering fingers, furled gracefully against the whispery texture of the elegant black chiffon skirt, ticked off his detestable qualities. He was domineering—arrogant—impatient—far too sure of himself, even when the entire sane world tried to convince him that he was wrong—withdrawn, stone-faced revealing nothing of his inner self while demanding that everyone else lay his or her emotions bare to be captured in the blinding flash of his camera.

She had run out of crimson-tipped fingers, but it was far too much trouble to start on the other hand. Anyone that despicable wasn't worth the effort it took to make the small movements required to go on enumerating his defects.

Casi let her eyes glide down the heaving length of the ferryboat's deck to the bow. At the moment he was neither stone-faced nor withdrawn. Merely obdurate. There he stood, all six-foot-four of him, wavy black hair in a thick, cyclone-tossed thatch from having his fingers dragged through it so often. He looked like one of his corsairing ancestors ordering someone flogged at the mast—or whatever it was those old Portuguese sea captains did with mutineers in the days when their authority reigned supreme on the high seas.

As she watched he flung wide his long, muscular arms, sending rippling sinews flexing up his back. Casi shivered and blamed the climate. The sleek blue Windbreaker did nothing to conceal his lithe strength—or the impatient movements indicating that he was still dissatisfied with the electricians' efforts. He was obviously determined to have the lighting manipulated to suit his rigid requirements if it took until midnight to position the floodlamps, the strobes, the thousand-candlepower spotlights that were supposedly going to simulate moonlight on this foggy bay. Casi had the impression he might at any moment grasp Luna in both powerful hands, wresting it out of orbit, to demonstrate exactly how the real thing ought to look.

He never shouted; she'd grant him that. He didn't need to. When Nicholas Penheiro quirked one of those black slashes he called eyebrows, people jumped— leapt, actually—to do his bidding.

They had all been bowing to his commands for six days now. Scavanging the city for precisely the right background in front of which to photograph each of Melina's breathtaking designs. Cable cars by day, Coit Tower by sunset, Maiden Lane by daffodils. Not to mention a swaying Golden Gate Bridge by wind-whipped night.

Well, she'd be darned if Casi Cavanaugh was going to leap one more time. Should she have had the slightest inclination in that direction—for no other reason than to finish this project and see the last of him—she couldn't have managed it. She was simply too exhausted to move.

Drooping back against the puffy, beanbag-type cushions that had been piled high against a bulkhead to give her a modicum of support, Casi allowed the thickly mascaraed eyelashes to flutter down across her cheeks. Even if the cushions had permitted it she was too much of a professional to actually collapse, though her aching body had been nagging her to do so for the past two hours. No, that might disarrange her carefully structured hairdo, mar the creamy blending of her makeup, or—perish the thought—crease a sixteenth-of-an-inch wrinkle in the perfectly pressed, exquisitely patterned evening gown she wore. If that happened, they would have to start all over again. The entire party would be aboard this creaking Flying Dutchman until Alcatraz became the official Northern California Disneyland.

It felt wonderful to close her eyes. Not to have to worry about imbuing their emerald depths with a pay-attention-to-me-folks sparkle. Not to be required to focus them into a sincere and warmly enticing gaze, so that whoever caught sight of her paper image would be stimulated to line up, credit card in hand, to buy whatever she was currently being photographed to advertise. Perfume. Jewelry. Lipstick. Or this week, Melina Jorgensen's fabulous new line of clothing, to be dubbed "San Francisco Spectaculars."

A waft of scent, spiced carnations, merged subtly with the salt-tanged air. "Hi, Melina," Casi groaned without opening her eyes.

"You look beat," the designer sympathized. "I'm sorry this is taking so long. By now I had visions of all of us safely back ashore, tucked cozily into our little beds at the Mark Hopkins."

"Forget it. He's determined that none of us will ever sleep again."

Without conscious volition, Casi raised her heavy eyelids. Her gaze traveled again to the towering figure at the vessel's bow. He stood arms akimbo now, feet planted like the roots of a Sequoia in a sinuous jungle of extension cords coiled along the planked deck. Urging. Cajoling. Demanding the utmost and more from the hapless electricians. She sighed, picturing hot food, relaxing brandy, a feathery pillow—all of which were totally out of reach for hours yet.

Turning her gaze back to the slender, raven-haired woman who for years had been her best friend, she asked the question that had been uppermost in her mind all week.

"How could you stand him while you were growing up?"

"I worshipped him. He could make me do anything—and love it." Melina's warm brown eyes glowed with the memory. "He was five years older. I was baby sister, a tiny Maid Marion trotting along behind Robin Hood, carrying the Band-Aids. Nicholas was Jack the Giant Killer, St. George about to slay the dragon, Richard the Lion-Hearted."

"The Marquis de Sade."

"Never! I'll admit he's grown a shell and dragged it over him the past few years, but it is simply not in his nature to be deliberately cruel to anyone or anything. If you could have seen him caring for the birds along the shore after that oil spill . . ."

Melina splayed beringed fingers, begging for understanding. "Nicholas was always carrying on crusades. Maybe it's time he found a new cause. He's just a perfectionist, Casi. And a man who's hiding. Nowadays he keeps his finer qualities tamped down and out of sight so no one can get close enough to guess how truly vulnerable he is. Once you get to know him—"

"I don't want to get to know him. I just want to escape from his clutches. He's impossible!"

"You'd be a marvelous pair. Fire and ice."

In spite of her fatigue Casi found herself laughing. "Don't let the red hair fool you. I'd need to be ten years younger to fuel the kind of blowtorch required to melt that glacier your brother has fused around himself!"

"You're only thirty-one. The same age as me, and think where my career has gone in the past year. Up, up, up. Between your look and Nicholas's photography, we're going to steal the fashion scene away from Paris and New York. The sky will be the limit!"

Casi groaned and closed her eyes again. "While you're up there, look around and find me a nice, laid-back astronaut, will you? It would be great to just float weightlessly around in space for a while. More and more the quiet life is beginning to appeal to me."

I CAN'T ABIDE THAT WOMAN, Nicholas thought. Stubborn—opinionated—argumentative—career-oriented to the hilt—and a damned distraction!

As if to underline this last failing, he felt his eyes straying once again from the work he was supervising. His dark glance speared down the length of the boat to skewer the woman propped up against those yielding cushions. She looked like a puppet, he decided, waiting to be told where, how and when to move next. Without a doubt, her entire world revolved around appearing beautiful twenty-four hours a day. Which, when you came right down to it, was a fashion model's only reason for existence.

And demanding! Insisting on breaks for the crew and herself of course, whether the light was fading or not. Soft. She didn't seem able to withstand the slightest hardship. Not that he cared whether she withstood anything. Ever.

Only the day before he'd had her lack of substance more than adequately demonstrated to him. Impatient

with all the delays, he had grabbed her arm, pulled her
toward him—merely to show her exactly where he
wanted her to stand on the bridge. The milky white skin
had felt like silk under his fingers. And when a gust of
wind had chosen that moment to hit the girders on
which they were standing, she had practically blown
into his arms. No stamina. No endurance. Six feet tall,
yet bowing to a puff of breeze. She had swayed, brac-
ing herself with her heels, her blazing green eyes defy-
ing him to steady her. Yet the shimmering auburn
tresses had flung themselves at him, curling for one
tantalizing instant about his face and neck like something warm, fiery, alive.

What misplaced sense of loyalty made Melina insist
that this woman and no other should be the one to
launch her new fashion line he would never understand. Bringing her all the way from New York simply
because they were friends and one-time roommates was
ridiculous; there were hundreds of younger, equally
gorgeous models arriving on the fashion scene an-
nually. He had been seeing that oval face with its uptilted nose and damnably kissable lips on magazine
covers and in four-color advertisements for more years
than he could count. She had to be much older than she
looked, which was about nineteen right now. It was
incredible, the way her long, curvaceous body molded
itself to the cushions! How she could be so light that the
breeze could move her, and still be so fantastically well-
rounded?

Well, she was Melina's friend, not his. He only had
to endure one more day of her distracting presence.
Less, if they could get this hideously intricate setting
right sometime before daybreak.

Much as he loved his sister, he should not have let her
talk him into attempting this job, Nicholas grumbled

to himself. Except for a few occasions early in his career when he had needed ready money quickly, he had never been a fashion photographer. He was used to catching real things in his lens—the plight of a child trapped in the rubble of a bombing, the desperate faces of hostages menaced by terrorists. More recently his subjects had been whales and baby seals, hunted almost to extinction by the greed and stupidity of modern man. Now here he was shooting some silly piece of fluff lounging around in a gown so expensive that the cost of it would feed a destitute family for a year!

However, since he had given in to his sister's pleas to be her cameraman, he was going to make sure the job was done right. Perfectly, in fact. This was Melina's big chance to achieve her lifetime ambition. She had spent years preparing for this moment, and he was going to do everything in his power to see that she attained that goal, even though it had meant being trapped for six interminable days in the world of high fashion.

But what was most aggravating at the moment was that Casi Cavanaugh had been right about the ferryboat. She had thrown up her hands in exasperation when he had conceived the idea of renting the thing for an evening, contending that the vessel was too awkward, too cumbersome, too poorly equipped for their purpose. What did she want—the *QE II*? His concept had been to picture Melina's wonderful designs with the lights of the city's skyline and the moonlit waters of San Francisco Bay behind them. It was a unique approach, a potential prizewinner. But all through their preliminary discussions, right up to the time they had put out to sea, that woman had continued to point out hazards, drawbacks, complications.

Surprisingly, for someone who had never used her brain to do more than select the most flattering shade of eye shadow, she had been correct in her assessment of the situation. This time he had gotten too ambitious. He could visualize the effect, but there seemed to be nothing he could do to make it come out the way he had planned. The lighting was still not right; it was too demanding a job for the technicians. They were used to working inside a studio, or at least on dry land, with numerous electrical outlets and a solid floor beneath them.

Instead, half a mile from shore on this heaving bay, they were becoming more and more ensnarled in a multitude of extension cords. The harder they attempted to make adjustments, the more hopeless it all looked. There were still shadows everywhere. The effect he was striving for simply would not work with that monumental defect spoiling everything.

There was only one measure they hadn't tried yet. With a scowl Nicholas stared at the ceiling, then swung back to the workmen, pointing out changes to be made. "Cluster the lights in closer," he snapped. "Group them there—and there. . . . Never mind about the cords right now. And bring that huge spotlight directly overhead. Focus it on the railing." At last the shadows were gone. Finally!

"We're ready," he called, dashing the sweat off his brow, anxious to be finished with this once and for all. "Let's get it on film!"

AT HIS SIGNAL Casi tipped her body upright. Good professional training did for a person what Pavlov did for his dog, she supposed. She took a deep breath, considering the fourteen long years she'd been in this business. *It's about time to quit while you're ahead, Casi my girl,* she told herself. She couldn't keep those crow's-feet at bay forever. Time to find some easy-going man and settle down to raising babies, give the real Casi Cavanaugh a chance to shine through, instead of just her paper image. Heaven knew she'd achieved enough success to last a lifetime.

She tensed her muscles isometrically, then allowed them to relax. That usually worked when she was feeling the strain of an exhausting job. This time, though, the effort only added to her fatigue.

One last season, she spurred herself on. Only one more—if he ever got it on film to his satisfaction—and she was finished with that handsome but ornery beast forever. She could sleep for a week!

The deck rocked underfoot as she picked her way down the rough planking toward the mastermind who had engineered this bit of dramatic imagery. She had to admit that his ideas were sound, even though the hastily rigged lights looked about as solid as the sea underneath this ancient hull. Watch him make it turn out fantastic in spite of all her dire predictions, she thought gloomily. But even though that would prove her wrong and him right, she wanted it to happen for Melina's sake.

Much as she hated to admit it, he was a genius with the camera. Way back—seven or eight years ago, when she and his sister had been splitting the rent on an expensive third-floor walk-up opposite Central Park—his work had excited her. Samples of it would arrive from Beirut, from Tehran, from Tel Aviv—all the trouble spots of the world—in long, cardboard-padded envelopes.

In those days she had been almost as anxious as Melina to tear open the flap and drag out those vivid, poignant photographs. Shots that other cameramen would have either ignored or botched were taken with such insight, such contrast and composition and precision that an amateur Polaroid user felt downright humble.

And since he had changed his life-style, buried himself in some waterside wilderness to concentrate on wildlife and ecology, his work had grown even more superb. Three books of his photos, accompanied by an incredibly sensitive text, had been produced so far. Each one was more outstanding than the last.

Those pictures had lured her out here. He, the man she had visualized him as being, had been the bait. That and her solid, long-term friendship with Melina. She couldn't turn down an appeal from a close friend any more than she could resist the notion of being photographed through the magic lens of Nicholas Penheiro.

What a disappointment had been in store for her! He had shown nothing but dislike for her since the moment they met. From the way he had been carrying on all week, she suspected he hadn't even wanted the assignment. He was just grudgingly fulfilling a family obligation.

The boat shuddered again. Casi thrust out her arms for balance, afraid that the narrow spike heels she was wearing to complement the sequin-bodiced evening gown would wedge in the cracks of the planking and throw her to the deck. She had almost fallen yesterday out on the bridge. Nearly barreled into his arms when his hand closed over her elbow, shooting lightning bolts up her spine. But then he had made some cutting remark and she had managed to catch herself just in time, inches short of colliding with that muscular chest. She hadn't mistaken the stiffening of his jaw, the gleam of mockery in those hooded black eyes. As though he were silently accusing her of clumsiness, or worse, deliberately hurling herself at him. Now, as then, she managed to maintain her equilibrium, righting herself and proceeding.

"Please stand against the railing," Nicholas directed curtly. "Try to look as if you're enjoying yourself. This setting is supposed to represent a 'dream-come-true' cruise ship, you know."

Casi wondered whether the camera would pick up the smoke that surely must be spiraling out of her ears right about now. While scarcely a cruise, it would be a dream come true for her if this intolerable boor fell overboard.

Because he was Melina's dearly beloved brother, and in the hope of getting this final session over with quickly, she kept her lips clamped tightly shut. Starting to move backward, she almost tripped over one of the cords that crisscrossed the deck in all directions. Stepping over it as gracefully as possible, she lounged back against the railing.

Nicholas eyed her with sardonic disdain. "Have you been condemned to walk the plank? I said enjoy yourself!"

There was no way her expression could be reflecting anything except annoyance with this abominable man at the moment, Casi realized. Never having been much of an actress, she found it extremely difficult to feign enjoyment while feeling none whatsoever. On a few other difficult occasions she had used the device of reverie to detach herself from the physical scene. At those times a fantasy picture flowing across her mind had put her in the mood for whatever it was her face was required to reflect.

She strove to conjure up an enjoyable daydream, and an image of Nicholas Penheiro being catapulted overboard rose mistily before her eyes. Down he would plunge, into the cold, dark water. He would flounder

there, that mahogany complexion turning blue. And—
her sense of humor began to respond to the image—
swimming toward him, a triangular fin on a sleek, gray
back.

Casi's lips parted in an ecstatic smile.

"That's it!" His voice encouraging, Nicholas spun
around, a dazzling Baryshnikov pirouetting on the edge
of this hideous pool of light, flashing the camera up and
down.

What grace, she thought. *A shame to let the shark
get it. However...*

"Terrific! Now dance, Casi. Swirl!" Nicholas
chanted. "Give yourself up to the romance of the evening. Make every woman who sees these photos absolutely yearn to wear that gown!"

Doing as she was bade, Casi arched her back, letting
her auburn hair flow across her shoulders. She
stretched out her arms enticingly, her emerald eyes
beaming an invitation to an invisible partner. On the
periphery of her vision Nicholas became Errol Flynn,
the master swordsman. A million points of light
bounced off the camera, like the glare of dazzling star-
bursts swirling around the tip of an épée.

"Dance!"

The shark would start low, nibbling on a toe first,
just to see what he tasted like. Her smile became downright rapturous. The mouth would open for a real bite
this time, and those big, sharp teeth—

"Wonderful!"

Totally enthralled by her unprecedented coopera-
tion, Nicholas slid across the splintery deck on one
knee. He aimed the camera, hardly hearing its rapid
whirr, flung himself sideways, catching more shots. He
leapt to his feet, focusing first on one side, then the

other. The camera's motion was continuous, capturing every nuance of her expression on them.

Melina was right, he admitted to himself. Casi was absolutely magnificent. He found himself wanting to crush this woman in his arms.

He strode backward, intent on a long view now. Something snagged, binding him, snaring his ankle. Preoccupied, determined not to miss a single flicker of Casi's wonderfully radiant smile, he yanked his leg, trying to free it without looking down.

At that precise moment a wave struck the ferryboat. Already off-balance, Nicholas went sprawling across the deck and the slithering black extension cord, tightened into a brutal knot. The violence of Nicholas's motion sent it snaking toward him, still clutching his flesh in its coiling trap.

The entire scenario had been played out in a fraction of a second. Melina's scream was the first warning Nicholas had of what was happening. Flat on his back, he twisted his body, staring up in horror. Overhead, the enormous spotlight tilted. The cord that anchored it to the ceiling was now taut and quivering, one end snarled around his foot.

The monumental globe creaked, tipped, pitched forward.

"Casi, look out!" Nicholas shouted, unable to move, powerless to shield her.

The crash was followed by a shattering explosion. Like darts propelled by a thousand blowguns, shards of glass blasted upward, sideways and out . . . toward the railing!

2

JUST AS THE STARCHY RUSTLE of the morning nurse's uniform was more stiffly crackling than that of her counterpart who came on duty at three in the afternoon, so Casi had learned to differentiate between the opthalmologist and any of the other doctors who occasionally entered her room. His garments made no sound at all, being most often, she suspected, the limp green garb worn in operating rooms. Yet he had an odd way of walking, a very slight hesitation between steps, as though one leg were a trifle stiff.

"Hello, Dr. Harvey," she said.

"You're getting very sharp."

"Like the scalpel you use when you're not wielding that lazer gizmo."

His voice was resonant, relatively young. The limp, she decided, must have come from an injury, rather than from a debilitating ailment such as arthritis. But concentrating on the sounds which made him unique in her ears was merely a postponement, and Casi knew it. She took a deep breath, steeling herself to pose the most tormenting question of her entire life.

"Well . . . have you brought good news or bad?"

"The stitches are out, and your two weeks of immobilization are up," he answered cautiously. "Now it's time to get your muscles back in shape. You're going to start walking around. Enjoy some exercise and fresh air for a change, while the healing process continues."

Casi inched her head toward the sound of his voice. Her hair felt slippery against the muslin on which she lay. They were allowing her to use a pillow now, which was an improvement. "I don't think you really answered my question, did you?"

The chair creaked as he settled into it. Cool fingers picked up her wrist, impersonally measuring her pulse.

"I won't be able to do that for another three weeks yet," Dr. Harvey said. "Your eyes must remain tightly covered during that entire time if the effect we're striving for is to be achieved. The best news, of course, is that we're going to allow you to go home. We want you to start leading as normal a life as possible, under the circumstances."

Three weeks! Casi withdrew into the pillow, shrinking down in frustration. How could she wait, not knowing, for what seemed an incredible length of time? How could she sustain hope, sanity? Wondering, for yet another twenty-one days, whether a life of utter blackness was to be her lot forever?

"Home to New York?" she whimpered, dodging that issue.

"Tired of me so soon? No, not to New York. Altitude is taboo for young ladies with bandages over their eyes. Besides, I'll want you close by in case something unforeseen should arise. I meant home with your friends." The voice sounded gently encouraging. "Up the coast, to their sea ranch. They're very anxious to have you come."

Casi's long body went rigid in the bed. "No! I don't want their pity!"

The doctor cleared his throat. "Guess I must have misunderstood. They aren't really your friends, after all," he observed, curling the words up into a question mark. "You don't actually care about them, I gather."

Casi made an impatient gesture, resenting his impli-
cation. "Melina's been my friend for years. Of course I
love her! She's sweet and kind and thoughtful. Her
husband is nice, too. I haven't known Dane nearly so
long, but he's a most pleasant man."

"And her brother? Nicholas?"

"That chauvinistic cameraman? I don't like him.
Definitely not!"

"That's good. Then you won't mind if he lives with
this burden of guilt for the rest of his life."

There was a drawn-out silence. "Oh, boy," Casi
breathed at last. "I figured you wore surgeon's green.
Don't tell me that under that wrinkled tunic beats the
heart of a psychiatrist."

"Hardly Sigmund Freud. But most doctors are keen
listeners, regardless of their uniform or specialty. You
talked about him a great deal while you were under
sedation."

"Oh, no." She caught her breath. "What did I say?"

"Ramblings, mostly. Something about a shark."

That was okay. For the first time in two weeks, Casi's
mouth tilted upward a millimeter. She had forgotten
about that little fantasy. "It wasn't . . . it's not really
pertinent. What were you saying about guilt?"

"Think about it. How would you expect him to feel?"

"Terrible, I guess." She had been so busy trying to
blot out memories of that ghastly event during every
waking moment that it had never occurred to her to
consider how the accident might have affected anyone
else. "If I had done this to another human being, I'd be
suicidal with remorse," she admitted unwillingly.

"That's a pretty fair description of his state of mind."

Dr. Harvey got up and limped around the room. He
paused somewhere, probably at the window, Casi decided. Occasionally one of the nurses had made a noise

from that direction; it had sounded like the slats of a
Venetian blind being adjusted. A week ago his words
would have made her glad that Nicholas was suffering, but most of her physical pain had receded by now.
In her case, misery didn't want any company.

"He shouldn't feel like that," she muttered. "It was
just a stupid accident."

"What happened was a terrible trauma for everyone
involved," the doctor's voice responded from a distance. "The two of you were literally covered with
blood the night the ambulance brought you to the hospital. Hours later, several people gave me their ver-
sions of what had taken place. Your friend and her
husband made a gallant effort to accept part of the
blame. But I don't think there's a doubt in anybody's
mind whose fault it really was. This man, Nicholas
Penheiro, was in a state of near collapse by the time you
came out of the operating room. He insisted on taking
full responsibility."

Both of them covered with blood? Had he been injured, too? She refused to ask. "Well, he should," she
said stubbornly. "It *was* his fault!"

"No question about it." The doctor's voice grew more
robust as he approached the bed and sat down again.
"He kept going over and over every detail of that horrible business with the extension cords, castigating
himself."

Casi didn't want to hear any more on that subject. It
wasn't her concern. It seemed to her that Dr. Harvey
was subtly transferring some of the responsibility for
Nicholas's guilt onto her own shoulders, and she was
simply not willing to accept the burden. She was the
one who had been the innocent victim!

Swallowing waves of emotion, she turned her head toward him. "What would you say my chances are? Truthfully."

"Truthfully?" He knew she was referring to her chances of seeing again. "Slightly better than half, I would estimate. The new techniques we used for your surgery are good, but hardly guaranteed. Call it sixty-forty. The edge is in your favor. But either way, no more modeling, I'm afraid."

She brought her fingertips up to touch her face. "Is it . . . really horrible?"

Gently the doctor pulled her hands away. "I'm not talking about scars. What few cuts you have will fade into practically invisible white lines very quickly. Even in front of a camera, a light speck of makeup would completely erase them. You aren't going to be disfigured, Casi, but you would never be able to tolerate working under glaring lights again, or having flashbulbs batter your eyes hour after hour."

Dr. Harvey sighed, as though in distress. "I'm being as honest with you as I can be," he added. "It's best that you start getting used to the idea. Begin making other plans for the future."

Her lips twisted wryly. "Funny you should mention that. Not ten minutes before the—the crash I'd been telling myself it was time to quit while I was ahead. I had visions of settling down to motherhood, raising a brood of nice, pink babies. I guess I'd better jettison that plan, too."

"Motherhood could be a great career," he said seriously. "Especially when you've already experienced more glamour and success than most women outside Hollywood ever get to taste."

So her modeling career had ended with a bang, Casi thought. Literally. As for the other life-style that had once seemed so appealing, no man was going to want a blind wife. And babies had a right to mothers who could see them.

"It would be easier if I were allowed to cry."

"I don't recommend it. You'd just get the bandages soggy, and Annabelle would be annoyed." She heard the chair legs scrape as he rose again. "In a few minutes she's going to come in and help you out of bed. Give you a bit of practice in walking around. You should be starting to use all those lazy muscles again. Be prepared for some dizziness at first. That should pass very quickly, however. By the day after tomorrow you'll be ready to leave here."

He hadn't gone. Casi could picture him standing there with his hands in his pockets, waiting for her to say something. Tenacious devils, doctors. She knew perfectly well what he wanted to hear.

"If I can't go home to New York, what are my other alternatives—besides the one you mentioned?" she asked.

"A convalescent home. There are several good ones here in the city. Mostly filled with the very elderly and the terminally ill. Possibly a hotel. But even if we sent a nurse along, that would be an extremely tedious existence for you. You need to start being around people again. Doing things. Talking. Laughing. Or, as I said, you do have the opportunity to make life a little easier for someone else."

"Fat chance. All they'd be doing is baby-sitting."

"Well, think it over." His uneven steps moved toward the door. She heard the faint click of the knob as it turned under his hand, but still he refused to depart.

"It's the strangest thing about that shark," he mused aloud. "You brought it up again and again. Each time you began mumbling about the creature you started by rooting it on. Urging it to go ahead and take a bite out of the photographer. Then, within a minute or two, you would become highly agitated. Scream desperately for Nicholas to swim away before he was injured." What sounded like a chuckle rumbled in Dr. Harvey's throat. "If I were a shrink instead of a surgeon, I could probably conjure up all sorts of interesting possibilities buried in that situation."

This time he did leave. Casi intercepted a little rush of air as the door swung open, then closed again with a semisilent thock of the latch. Her face felt hot as if color swirled around below the bandage, staining her cheeks with a blush.

Damn that shark, she thought. Damn the medication for loosening her tongue to such a degree, causing her to say things out loud that would never have crossed her lips had she been in her right mind. And double damn the doctor for eavesdropping on her demented ramblings, tattling on her subconscious to her, bringing out impossible emotions! Feelings that should be corked up and left, like a bottle of wine, to mist over with cobwebs in the deepest cellars of her mind.

It was a shock having to own up to those sentiments. Thinking about Nicholas had been much less difficult when she was firmly on the shark's side.

Almost eight years ago she and Melina and a couple of off-Broadway actresses had begun sharing the New York apartment. It was a convenient and economical way for a group of aspiring career girls to live. They took one another's messages, borrowed clothes, swapped dates, confided secrets. Eventually one of the actresses got married, and the other gave up and moved back to Wyoming. But by then she and Melina were making enough money to afford the place on their own. They had become as close as sisters.

They used to make popcorn—low-cal, without butter—and talk about everything under the sun. Often, their families.

Melina kept a large photograph of Nicholas on her dresser alongside those of her parents and grandparents and other assorted relatives. Casi had flipped over him the very first time she saw him. That wavy black hair and his strong, smiling face did things to her imagination. To her temperature.

It was sort of like having a bad crush on an unattainable movie star, though. He was already married. And at the time he was a renowned free-lance news photographer who spent most of his time out of the country. He didn't even like New York.

Considering the in-again, out-again type of lives they all led, it wasn't too curious that on each of the three visits he had made to the Big Apple to see Melina, she herself was away. Modeling swimsuits in Bermuda once. Skiing in the Adirondacks on the second occasion. The third time she was off on a weekend to Atlantic City when he made a trip back to the States from the Middle East. Returning to the apartment, she had learned to her great disappointment that he had departed no more than half an hour earlier.

It was about that time—four years ago, as close as she could remember—that his wife had been killed. The details were never clear. Something to do with terrorists. Mulling it over now, Casi wondered whether that was what had triggered the radical change in his lifestyle. Because right afterward he had dropped out of the international news scene entirely.

Melina had gone home to California a year later to start her own design studio, but she and Casi had kept up an enthusiastic correspondence and stayed in touch by phone. It was only natural that Casi should hear snippets about Nicholas just in passing. She began seeing his wildlife and ecology photographs in some of the same magazines that had formerly carried his action shots. Then his books came out, one by one, and she collected them. All three of them were back in her apartment right now. In a place of honor on the coffee table.

Casi wondered whether she would ever be able to look at them again. Even if she wanted to, which she didn't. Tears started to well up underneath the bandages, and she suppressed them vehemently. Those were the kind of maudlin thoughts she was supposed to avoid. It was better to go back to thinking about Nicholas now that she had started. If she concentrated hard enough on the reality of the man, rather than as how she had imagined him for all those years, maybe she could cleanse her system of him.

When the opportunity had arisen to come out and meet Melina's big brother in person, she had ruthlessly canceled other jobs, nearly wreaking total havoc on her agency. But for a chance to work with Nicholas Penheiro she'd have gone into competition with TWA and flapped her wings all the way to the West Coast. Recalling that smiling picture, the empathy in his work, she had expected someone warm and kindhearted—at least friendly.

He hadn't been any of those things. Just standoffish. Curt, stiff, almost rude. Definitely demanding. As though he had something against her personally. He had dragged her here and shoved her there and never said one pleasant word the whole time. His dark eyes had actually glittered with antagonism every time he looked at her. Apparently he hated fashion models. She had never figured out why. It was an honorable profession. Refusing to be intimidated, she had gotten her back up and responded just as coldly. By that final night, the evening of the ferryboat fiasco, daggers were flying every time their glances crossed. That, of course, was why she had dreamed up the shark.

And now she was supposed to do him a favor. Let him lead her around by the hand because it was his fault she couldn't see. Be an object of charity to alleviate some of his guilt. Ha!

Against the black velvet darkness that had replaced vision, she kept picturing his expression after he had sprawled to the deck. The scene would be forever frozen in her mind. He had looked up, horrified, then swung his head toward her. As though he wanted to sprint across the plankings and protect her. In that moment he was a different Nicholas entirely. But he couldn't get his foot loose, so he'd shouted, instead.

Because of that yell she had almost dived out of the way in time. Almost. That look on his face was the last thing she had seen. Maybe the last thing she would ever see.

Like her career, her eyesight had ended with a bang.

The door opened and closed. She heard a crackly rustling similar to a bowl of Rice Krispies when the milk was just poured over them and caught the powerful scent of nearby roses.

"Good morning, Annabelle," Casi said, glad of the interruption. "More flowers, I smell."

"They're in lieu of the visitors you haven't been able to have," the early-shift nurse replied. "Starting today, though, people will be allowed to drop in for a few minutes at a time. Do you want to keep these, or shall I parcel them out like the rest of the bouquets you've been getting every day?"

"What does the card say?"

"It's signed, 'With love from Melina, Dane and Nicholas.'"

"Oh, leave them here this time." Casi sighed. "I don't care. Geriatrics and pediatrics and maternity are probably sick of all those long-stemmed buds by now."

The nurse's voice came across the room. "I'm going to put them over here on the ledge so you won't be cavorting into them. Dr. Harvey says you can get up and take a stroll today. What do you think about that?"

"Anything beats bedpans," Casi said frankly. "He also warned me about dizziness, so let's take it easy."

Rubber-soled feet approached. Then Annabelle was tugging at her shoulders, propping her upright. Casi clung to the plump arm, experiencing a sudden wave of nausea. "Oh, that's awful! I can't—"

"Yes, you can. Hold on."

In time the whirling images in her head receded and the buzzing in her ears diminished. "I'm sure glad we don't have to do this with an audience," she choked, wondering if she was going to be sick, hoping the detested bedpan was nearby. Cold beads of perspiration coated her upper lip as the nurse dragged away the covers and helped her swing her legs over the side of the bed.

"Put your hands here on the post and hang on while I get your robe. Try taking deep breaths."

In a minute nubby terry cloth slid over her shoulders. It was an effort to push her arms through the sleeves. Her body felt as limp as a strip of taffy that has been left lying on a windowsill in the sun. Casi tried wiggling her toes and ankles to get some life back into them. Then the floor came up and smacked her.

She buckled at the first step and had to sink back onto the mattress. In five minutes they tried it again. This time she made it four feet, windmilling the arm Annabelle wasn't clutching, before her knees went.

"Would you believe I used to ski the pro slopes at Aspen? Gallop through Central Park with the mounted police every Saturday? Do peppers at jump rope?" she moaned, embarrassed by her rubbery limbs.

In half an hour the nurse allowed her to sit in a chair while she changed the bed linen. Crisp, unwrinkled sheets had never felt so glorious, Casi thought, slipping back between them.

"After two weeks of just lying here, fretting to get up, I never thought I'd be so glad to feel this mattress under me again," she panted.

"I'll give you a break. You can sleep for an hour. After lunch we'll try it again. Then it will be time to have your bath and get dolled up for company."

"Just because the sign says Visiting Hours doesn't mean anybody will show up."

"Sure it does," Annabelle said cheerfully. "Believe it or not, there's been someone here for you every single day. Your girlfriend, always. Usually a man, too. Big, tall fellow."

Casi's fingers stilled against the raised pattern of the spread. "Black-haired or blond?"

"Very dark. Looks like a matador. Umm. Wish he'd come and see me."

"Believe me, Annabelle, you'd be safer with the bull!"

THE SECOND EXERCISE SESSION wasn't nearly so bad. Tottery, but a definite improvement. Feeling fresh after her bath, Casi meekly submitted to having her hair brushed and the bandage over her eyes changed. During this process Annabelle darkened the room to the deepest possible degree. Nevertheless she warned her patient to keep her eyelids firmly closed. Obeying, Casi still felt a throb of disappointment as the blackness remained complete when the padded cloth was lifted away. Not a glimmer of light penetrated the obsidian blank she had become accustomed to. Had there been any cause for hope, surely she would have noticed some difference when the blindfold was removed!

"Quit rushing things." The nurse read her expression correctly. "That process takes time to work. Didn't Dr. Harvey explain that you aren't supposed to see for a while yet? When your eyes are ready they'll come around."

The bandage was replaced. Though just as uncompromisingly wrapped, this one felt smaller. Probably for the sake of cosmetology, Casi thought, since they were about to throw open the gates and let outsiders in to goggle at her.

She reminded herself that the outsider would be Melina, who had seen her with mumps. No point taking this out on her. Something would have to be done about her own attitude.

"Do I look more like a raccoon or the Lone Ranger?" she asked flippantly.

"Like Brenda Starr playing peekaboo with Basil's eye patch." Annabelle wasn't the kind to take any cheek from a mere patient, but her touch was kind as she slipped a lacy bed jacket over Casi's shoulders and gave her long, auburn hair a final glide with the brush.

"There!" she said. "You're ready for your public."

"Just one little piece of that public," Casi said firmly. "If Mrs. Jorgensen is here, I'd like to see—I wouldn't mind having her come in. But nobody else."

"You're crazy." Annabelle sighed and went to open the door.

"It's only me," Melina said in a small, timid voice. "Nicholas has gone back downstairs to wait."

Casi tried out a smile. "I know. Spiced carnation perfume, unaccompanied by the brute's Brut."

"We've—I've been wanting to come, but they'd never let me through the door."

"I wouldn't have been very good company." Casi shrugged. "They didn't allow me to talk or move around until the stitches were out. Today, though, the nurse had me up, practically dancing in the aisles. I think she and the doctor are really tired of me. They're evicting me in a couple of days."

Melina caught her breath. "That's wonderful. You're coming home with us, of course."

"The bed jacket feels great. And thanks for all the flowers, too. I shared with half the hospital. What did you do—buy out Podesta-Baldocchi?"

"The roses were from Nicholas. Just the bed jacket was my idea. It's beautiful on you, Casi. Kind of a seafoam green, with lots of lace."

There was a series of tiny clicks, as though rings were clashing from hands being twisted together. "Listen, about Monday. . . Dane can take the day off work and make sure we get you home safely. It isn't as if you had to depend on my rotten driving to take you across the bridge. He'd be glad to do it. You won't have to see—I mean, Nicholas wouldn't need to—"

"Hey, don't cry, Melina. Please!" Casi held out her hand. Instantly two big, warm drops splattered across it.

"My imbecile tongue simply won't behave. I've been rehearsing what I wanted to say to you all week, and now everything's come out wrong!"

Melina was becoming more and more distressed. Wanting to calm her, Casi could only flap her hands helplessly.

"I'm not going to have hysterics again. I'm not," Melina choked. "That horrible night I thought I was going to lose not only my best friend, but my brother, too. Nicholas nearly went out of his mind, Casi. That's the truth. I've never seen him look so tormented, not even when Mother died. He yanked his foot out of his shoe and ran through all that splintered glass, and grabbed you up in his arms as if you were a rag doll. He was holding you against his chest and your blood was all over—all over both of you—"

She was gulping and sobbing, thrusting the jagged words through her lips with an emotion that tinged on desperation. Casi drew a shuddering breath, feeling tears streaming down her own cheeks underneath the bandage.

"Dammit, Melina, shut up, will you? I'm not supposed to cry!" she bawled. "I know it must have been terrible for—for everyone that night. Was the dress a total loss? Did—did the pictures come out all right, at least?"

Her chest heaved and her throat was aching from the gigantic effort she was making to hold back the rest of her unshed tears. She was hurling words out every which way, trying to think of something to say that would relieve the tension, saying anything—anything—to get the subject away from Nicholas. It was so excruciatingly unfair to think that when he had finally taken her in his arms she wasn't even conscious to enjoy it!

Melina ripped a tissue out of the bedside box and blew furiously. "The pictures were fine. Gloriously beautiful. The line is selling like— What difference does that make?" Casi felt a dab of a tissue trembling against her own cheek, blotting up tears. "The hell with high fashion and photographs and everything else right now! You're what counts—getting you well!"

"Gimme one of those," Casi snuffled, holding out her hand. She blew her nose, resolving to put an end to this emotional scene. "Lord, I envy men at times like these," she said a little less shakily. "You wouldn't catch them breaking down and bawling."

"They'd be better off if they did, instead of holding it all inside." Melina sounded somewhat calmer, too. Still close to the edge, though. "I wailed like a banshee for days, but Nicholas—Nicholas never said one word after we left the hospital. He's still going around looking like death. It scares me, Casi. I'd consider it a huge favor if you'd come on home with us and let him try to make it up to you."

"I don't want sympathy!" The words tore from her throat like a desperate appeal.

Melina took three or four big gulps of air. "Then we'll make sure you don't get any," she declared. "Just a lot of friendship and moral support. I swear to you, nobody will even say they're sorry. It's a huge spread, you know. There are two houses on the grounds. Nicholas lives acres away. You wouldn't have to—to talk to him at all if you didn't want to. He'll stay at his own place most of the time. Unless . . ."

"Unless what?"

"Unless you were willing to let him help. I think it would be good for both of you."

"Well, you said he was ready for another crusade," Casi replied bitterly. "Maybe I'm destined to be it."

"Call it anything you want," Melina whispered. "Just say you'll come."

Casi turned her head away, feeling as though her entire soul were being ripped into shreds. The request had sounded poignantly humble, and humility had never been one of Melina's virtues. She was one of life's battlers. But maybe she was still battling, just using a different tone of voice to do it in. Nicholas must be in a very bad way, indeed, to evoke this kind of pleading from his sister.

Remembering the doctor's words, Casi tried to picture how she would react if she were responsible for something terrible having happened to him. She had felt so guilty for even fantasizing about a shark eating him that she had babbled about it while under sedation. That was an entirely different case, of course. There was a time when she'd had a terrible crush on him.

Old crushes ought to count for something, she supposed.

"I'll come," she surrendered. "And don't make Dane take off work, either. It doesn't matter who comes to pick me up. I'll be ready."

3

THE WHEELCHAIR RIDE down the elevator from the hospital's upper floor, through the buzzing lobby and out to the curb had been dizzily disorienting. Casi's head was still spinning as she wavered on the sidewalk. She felt an ominous sense of chill that had little to do with the last vestiges of morning fog still lingering in the atmosphere.

There was a sound of small rubber wheels making a U-turn across the cement. "By, Miss Cavanaugh!" the candy striper's voice drifted back to her, blending with the streetside traffic noises.

Resting her hands on the smooth, dewy roof of the car, Casi waited, trying to appear more placid than she felt. She hoped her face wore a look of composure, but doubted that this was the case. Inside she was a seething mass of turmoil. Between Dr. Harvey and Melina she had been railroaded into this situation. She had the distinct and most uncomfortable impression that her destiny had been snatched out of her own control and placed in the charge of others.

Following instructions, she ducked awkwardly inside. The back seat was wide, deep, covered in a velvety plush that cushioned her in opulent comfort. Tentatively she stretched out her feet. Yards of leg room. Definitely not someone's basic Volkswagen.

"Watch your hands, please," a deep, neutrally toned voice said not far from her ear. It sounded as though the speaker were bending toward her, withholding the door's closing until he was positive she had no intention of leaping out again. Which, of course, was exactly what she yearned to do.

Casi tensed, tucking arms and elbows and fingers around in front of herself, keeping everything rigidly out of harm's way. A rush of cold air struck her, and she heard the uncompromising thunk of metal against metal. Spreading her hands wide as they curled toward her sides, she fumbled for the two halves of the seat belt.

Melina had slid into the car first and positioned herself behind the driver's seat to make Casi's entry easier. Hearing the little intake of breath to her left, Casi could picture her friend biting her lip, restraining herself until she was sure her help was needed.

Another blast of damp air gushed its way inside as the driver's door opened. The car dipped, receiving his weight. She felt a vibration as that door, too, was pulled tightly closed. But there was no click yet of key being joined with ignition switch, only the bump of motion up front, as though he had swiveled around to watch what she was doing.

Casi tried to ignore the fact that they were both observing her. *One thing at a time*, she thought, forcing herself to pay complete attention to the small task she had set for herself. Was the belt a hook type or shove-in clasp? Her fingers investigated the smooth metal tips of the safety device. She could feel them tremble against her lap, betraying her anxiety to pass this first, crucial test of semi-independence. Shove-in, she decided.

Concentrating hard, she pointed the two ends at each other and felt her right hand cross futilely over the left. Missed by a mile! Her jaw tightened. She brought her hands apart again. The second time when she pushed the belt forward she raised two of her opposite fingers to act as a barrier against overshooting the mark so widely. Again the right end slid on top of the left, but because of the guard she had erected, she was able to back it up a few inches and make a relatively easy adjustment. One end of the belt clicked satisfyingly inside the other. She let it go and tightened the canvas strap around her midsection.

From beside her came a small sound of relieved respiration. Melina had been holding her breath. Casi turned toward her, hearing a tremor of stress in her own voice. "One gold star for my report card. For a minute there I was afraid I'd have to settle for *A* for effort."

"I'm really impressed," Melina gulped. "I'm quite sure I couldn't have done that."

"You'd be surprised what you can do when you have to."

For the sake of everyone's morale, Casi knew she was going to have to get this business of at least seeming to communicate with him over as quickly as possible. "That's Nicholas in the front seat, right?" she asked, trying to make it sound casual. As if identifying one's driver from behind a blindfold were an everyday occurrence. "I appreciate your coming to get me."

It was as much as she could manage, but the few words seemed to break the tension.

"I'll try to drive smoothly," he replied after an infinitesimal pause. "It will be city and highway traveling for a while, but the last part of the road is bumpy. We'll warn you when it's time to brace yourself."

Casi felt a grateful squeeze on her left wrist—Melina saying thank-you in her own discreet way. Casi was glad she had made the effort to acknowledge Nicholas's presence. At least the first hurdle was over.

All morning Casi had been trying to block him out of her thoughts. She had been awake for hours, since long before dawn, judging from the pulse of hospital activities. Thinking. Trying to decide how best to behave. Most of it would have to be played by ear—literally. But she had already resolved to keep things light, not make waves and, most of all, stay out of everyone's hair as much as possible.

An enormous number of difficulties lay ahead, she knew. Just because she had surmounted one tiny challenge didn't mean the rest of them would be any easier to overcome. Without a doubt the coming three weeks would feel like three years, all told.

One thing Casi intended to insist on, after the first day or two of getting settled in, was that Melina continue her usual work schedule. Unless Casi missed her guess, a great deal of time in publicizing the new line had been wasted because of the traumatic chain of events following the last photography session. At this vital stage of the new fall-fashions launch every minute counted. They were already into March. Buyers would be making concrete plans to order their showrooms' cool-weather clothing. Fashion wasn't a last-minute thing; it required months of advance scheduling. Melina couldn't afford to take three weeks off to hold her hand.

It felt weird to be riding in a car and not able to look out the window. She had no way of telling how fast they were going or what kind of scenery was whizzing past. From the numerous pauses, she assumed they were on a stop-and-go boulevard, undoubtedly some route that would take them onto the bridge approach. Casi had visited San Francisco several times in the past. With all the dashing around recently in search of photography locales, she had become reacquainted with its most famous landmarks. But now she had no sense of direction at all. Her confusion increased when she realized she had not the slightest idea of where she had spent the last two-plus weeks. She didn't even have a starting point to reckon from. Nobody had thought to tell her the name of the hospital!

About to ask for the information, Casi squeezed her lips shut on the question. Whatever she said, it was sure to sound like a taunt to Nicholas. The mere mention of hospitals—or photographs, ferryboats, lights and heaven knew how many dozen other ordinarily innocent things—within his hearing was bound to imply some sort of accusation. As if she were subtly tormenting him, reminding him of the accident that had blinded her. Why provoke another skirmish, start the icicles dripping from his voice again? She'd rather stay uninformed than risk having her ears frostbitten.

The lengthening silence inside the car was becoming nervously oppressive. It was as if the others, too, were carefully guarding their tongues. Probably they were wondering what they could say to *her* that wouldn't be misinterpreted. If this kept up, Casi thought, about half the words in the English language were due to be shoved firmly back into the dictionary and left unspoken.

The engine's purr changed tempo, indicating a slight increase in their speed. The noise of intersection traffic diminished, and there weren't such constant pauses. At intervals Casi had a peculiar notion that the sound of their tires was ricocheting off some sort of baffle. Walls? Hills? Of course, hills. This city was full of steep ups and downs. But nearby, quiet hills?

"The Presidio?" she guessed out loud, then realized she had made it a question.

Next to her Melina jumped. "How did you know? You can't—"

"No, I can't. It was a process of elimination, that's all." Casi sighed. "I've been wondering where we are, and knew we had to be heading for the bridge. But there isn't enough noise for it to be Van Ness or Lombard, or enough stomach-turning dips for Divisadero. I haven't heard a cable car, and I think there are fewer traffic lights. Did I guess right?"

"Yes, of course it's the Army post," Melina said delightedly. "It's by far the most peaceful spot in the whole city. And the prettiest, too. Look how green—"

There was a hideously awkward pause.

In a spurt of exasperation Casi clenched her fists and pounded them on her knees. "Look how green everything is, now that spring is just around the corner!" she finished the sentence emphatically. "Or words to that effect. Isn't that what you meant to say? Then out with it, for heaven's sakes! Quit worrying about hurting my feelings!"

She ran an agitated hand over her forehead. "I was doing the same thing myself, not ten minutes ago, while I was groping for a sense of location. I didn't even know where we'd come from. Nobody had ever mentioned the name of the hospital to me. I wanted to ask, but I clammed up because I was afraid it would sound as if I were bringing up some awful memory on purpose."

Beside her Melina made a sound that could have been a muffled sob.

"Think about how much we've all said to one another since we started out," Casi went on relentlessly. "It hasn't exactly been a sparkling conversation, has it? Too many words are off-limits for comfort. Everyone's afraid to open his mouth for fear of sticking his foot in it. It's time we all quit being so tactful. Either that, or let me out right now. I'll bum a ride back to the hospital!"

From up front there came a noise of expelled breath. "You can't," Nicholas pointed out with irrefutable logic. "You don't know what the place is called. And I for one am not about to tell you."

"I'm afraid you're stuck with us, shoe-leather tongues and all," Melina said tremulously. "Casi, darling, bear with us, please. We'll get it smoothed out, I promise you."

Furtively Casi dashed away moisture from her cheeks. At least things were out in the open now. They knew how she felt. Maybe by the end of the third week she and Melina might even be talking naturally to each other again.

"Golden Gate coming up," Nicholas said in his best tour-guide diction. "Free direction, so we won't be stopping at the toll booth. After that we have a short way to go along 101. Then we'll be turning off to the left."

He nosed the car into the fast lane of the long suspension bridge. It was a brisk, clear morning now that the sun's radiance had burned off the fog. Whitecaps were lacing across the royal-blue surface of the bay. The city's skyline glistened in his rearview mirror, all tall rectangles and pyramids. He ignored the water and the greenery of Angel Island to the right, feeling his eyes drawn instead to a particular area of the massive amber-orange structure they were riding across. The girders over there were the ones he had finally chosen as the backdrop against which to photograph a smart gray-and-navy tweed suit. As then, this morning was on the breezy side. But of course, today nobody was swaying. The car's rigid steel exterior stood between them and the buffeting gusts.

When I'm wrong, I really go all out, he told himself in disgust, recalling how he had considered Casi weak for bowing to the wind's force. *She may look soft on the outside, but inside where it counts she's made of tensile steel.*

The shock of seeing her this morning when the wheelchair had deposited her on the curb had left him shaken and speechless, it hurt so much to look at her. Always slender, now she had the fragile delicacy of hand-blown glass. Curves still flowed beneath the loose fit of her jacket, but in considerably less rounded proportions. The contrast between the pallor of her face and the dark slash of material that masked her eyes was totally heart-rending. Were it not for the vivid auburn hair spilling across her shoulders, she'd have had the appearance of an ethereal spirit rather than that of an earthbound mortal. He had caused that look, that weight loss, Nicholas accused himself. He had done that to her.

And she was terrified of him. Scared to death he would come near her, hurt her again. He had caught that frightened doe look when she was getting into the car. If he had touched her she would have fled in panic, bolted out into the traffic. Automatically he had reached to take her hand, then frozen when he saw the tattered, half-healed cuts welted across it and up her wrist. That was why her face was so relatively unmarked. At the last minute she had flung up an arm to shield herself from the blast of shattering glass. If only she had raised it higher!

What a damnable waste, he thought miserably. Those sparkling emerald eyes ravaged, while he lay helplessly on the deck, trapped by the results of his own stupidity. He had seen the spotlight tip, had known that disaster was imminent. In that split second he realized what Casi meant to him. He had tried to untangle himself, to throw himself in the way, to safeguard her with his own body. But the cord had held, forcing him to watch in horror while she absorbed the fierce rain of splintering glass.

In that moment he would have gladly given his life to protect her. As he would now. But the proud tilt of her chin warned him to stand clear, to leave her alone. The seat belt business had demonstrated how determined she was to fight her own battles.

It was too late now to wonder why he hadn't seen her in this light before, rather than as the silly, useless mannequin he had desired with a passion that secretly terrified him. Nicholas had been asking himself that question for weeks. He ought to know by now there was simply no answer to it.

"Until I was seventeen, Papa used to have to stop constantly every time we traveled this road to let me out for fresh air," Melina confided artlessly. "These winding curves always made me carsick."

"I can understand why." Casi felt more than a little queasy herself. "Are we nearly there? It seems like an hour since we left the highway."

"Almost. Smell the salt in the air? Our property is just a mile or two north once this section of road reaches the sea and straightens out. It's a heavenly location. You'll love it, I know."

Casi knew better. She wasn't going to like any part of this ordeal. Especially now that she had finally admitted to herself how she felt about Nicholas. Having him so close, knowing he detested her, realizing it was only guilt that had put him into the same car with her had already made this journey seem endless.

"Isn't it a terribly long commute?" she protested. "Surely you don't make this trip morning and night five days a week?"

"That's the reason we kept Dane's old apartment downtown. As a rule the two of us stay there Monday through Friday, then head home," Melina explained. "It's like looking forward to a minivacation every weekend."

"Time to start holding on tight," Nicholas said abruptly. "We've reached the roughest part of the road. You're going to get bounced around pretty good back there."

And you'd hate to be responsible for having anything else happen to me, wouldn't you, Casi questioned him silently. She braced herself. The car lurched from side to side as ruts washboarded the tires. If only they would hurry up and reach their destination so she could get away from him!

He hadn't uttered more than an occasional syllable since they reached the turnoff. Yet she had been constantly aware of his presence there in the front seat. Once or twice she had caught a whiff of subdued aftershave. A few times she'd heard the rub of material across upholstery. She could picture his muscles rippling as he moved his arms and shoulders to swing into a turn.

Was he watching her disdainfully in the rearview mirror right now? Not likely. Probably he couldn't bear to look at her. Her presence had been forced on him, as his was on her. The kindest thing he could be thinking was that she was a burdensome nuisance. Well, he wasn't going to have to bother with her at all. She'd see to that.

For a moment he was dislodged from her seething thoughts when agitated barking loomed suddenly out of nowhere. Casi grabbed the seat cushions with both hands, aware that the bones must be showing whitely through her clenched knuckles. The shrill yelps grew louder and more demanding as the car slowed, then stopped. Nicholas's voice began issuing stern orders, starting with, "Scram!" There were a half-dozen thuds as leaping paws collided persistently with the door.

Casi's teeth started chattering; a film of perspiration speckled her upper lip. *Dogs,* she thought, feeling faint. *Ferocious animals, running loose!*

Melina noticed her tension. "Don't mind Gulliver," she said, laughing. "He just wants to hop in and slobber all over everybody. He'd win best of breed at face licking every time."

Surprisingly Nicholas addressed a question directly to her. "Have you ever had a dog, Casi?"

She shook her head, biting her lip in the hopes that she wasn't going to do anything stupid, such as passing out. "No. I'm a city girl, remember? He just startled me, that's all."

Nicholas knew panic when he saw it. A grenade suddenly tossed into the car would have frightened her less than the dog had. She hadn't had much practice in telling lies, he decided, feeling oddly pleased at the thought. Her face gave her away every time. Earlier in their acquaintance, when her eyes were visible, he had always known when she was struggling against the impulse to hit him. Even now it wasn't much harder to read her expression. Her skin was like chalk, totally drained of color. Her whole body was trembling.

First him, then the dog, he thought. Two unknown beasts. What a strain this blindfolded venture must be for her. He knew instinctively that she was close to the breaking point. They would have to be very, very careful to see that nothing taxed her beyond endurance.

"We've just passed Nicholas's house, which is really the old family homestead where we grew up," Melina said when the car had moved on. "Now we're coming up to our place—Dane's and mine. We started construction on the house shortly before we got married, but it isn't exactly completed yet. Dane wanted to do a lot of the finishing work himself, and I've been adding little touches here and there."

Casi jerked her thoughts away from whatever else might be lurking out there in the dark. "Sounds very satisfying," she murmured. "But I'll bet those mini-vacations are more work than play."

"Fun-work," Melina insisted. "As opposed to work-work like doing the dishes and designing clothes. We're here! Come on in and I'll show you around."

Fumbling with the seat belt, Casi heard the door being opened for her. She swung her legs around to the side and started to scoot out. Then her hand was clasped in a large, secure grip. The fingers were warm, engulfing. Her skin tingled at his touch. She had an insane impulse to give him the other hand to hold, too, then realized what a fool that would make her look. Casi the weakling, clinging to big, strong Nicholas. Wouldn't he sneer!

She jerked her hand away and hung on to the door, instead.

Nicholas's eyes clouded with pain at her rejection. "When my sister remarked that her home was not yet finished, she was particularly referring to landscaping," he said, determined at all costs to keep his voice from betraying any emotion. "Rubble would be too delicate a word to describe some of the area we will be passing. I think it would be best if you allowed me to assist you inside."

His words made her feel like an idiotic schoolgirl. Obviously he had no intention of being accountable for skinned knees or a twisted ankle on top of everything else.

"Perhaps you'd let me take your arm, then," she replied. The effort it cost to keep her voice impersonal didn't show, did it? "It's a little easier to keep my balance that way."

"By all means."

She felt the nudge of a suede-covered elbow brush her hand, indicating where she was to grab. Clamping her fingers around his powerful forearm, she held on and willed her wobbly knees to get moving. Why did he affect her like this? Why wouldn't her pulse quiet down, instead of pounding like a primitive tom-tom? *Walk*, Casi ordered herself.

"We'll be going up a gravel path for about forty feet and then ascending three low steps. I'll let you know when we reach the porch," Nicholas assured her.

She nodded, not replying. It wasn't all that far. She could do it. Mustering her confidence, she took one step, then another. She felt him hesitate, then match his paces to hers. The gravel crunched under the soles of her shoes. Trying hard to ignore him, she concentrated on her surroundings. The air was marvelous out here, she thought. Not a hint of smog. A brisk breeze was blowing, making her hair stream out every which way. Her nostrils caught the indefinable presence of the ocean not far away, mingled with the aroma of freshly sawed lumber.

Melina's footsteps had scooted on ahead. A key rattled in the lock, then there was the rapid swish of a door being flung open in welcome.

"Steps. Three of them," the man at her side warned.

Casi raised her foot and felt her toe stab hard against a wooden obstacle. She gasped, dragging at his arm, flinging her other hand forward in wild desperation, ready to brace herself in case she tumbled. Nicholas didn't allow that to happen. The crook of his elbow tightened over her fingers and his free arm darted out, pushing her shoulder back to keep her from falling.

"Damn!" he cursed softly. "It's not a very high step. I should have been more precise. You took about one and a half."

Quivering both from embarrassment at her clumsiness and from the effort of trying to treat this hideous situation with a nonchalance she was far from feeling, Casi stood rooted to the spot. Crawling up the stairs would be easier, but she wouldn't crawl. Not in front of him! She continued to hesitate, afraid to try it again.

"About six inches. I won't let you fall. Up!"

It was a voice he might have used on Gulliver: stern but encouraging. He ought to be running an obedience school, she thought, determined not to let him sense how shaky she felt. This whole morning had leapfrogged from stresspoint to stresspoint. Desperately she wished she could simply lie down and be left alone.

To her relief, Nicholas seemed bent on allowing her to do just that, and as quickly as possible. They had no more than reached the top of the steps, when she felt her fingers being removed from the suede sleeve and transferred over to his sister's gabardine-covered arm.

Melina stood still, allowing Casi time to make the adjustment. "You're not coming in, Nicholas?"

"No. I'll get her overnight bag out of the trunk and set it inside for you," he said. "Then I'll be heading on home. I daresay your guest could use a short breather."

Casi's chin trembled in humiliated fury. He couldn't wait to be rid of her. He was actually talking about her in the third person, as if she were some type of inanimate object.

"I'm just fine, Melina," she contradicted him haughtily. "I'd love to see—I'd love to hear all about your new house. Why don't we go inside?"

They stepped from a tile entryway onto a luxurious expanse of carpet. "The living room is really big. The front wall is all glass so we can watch the ocean from wherever we sit."

Melina's enthusiastic voice started mentioning details about stone fireplaces and redwood tables. Casi allowed the descriptions to flow past her as she listened to his angry-sounding footsteps recede, then quickly retrace their route up the path. There was a muffled thud as her small bag was dumped into the hall, followed by the subdued bang of the door.

Instantly her shoulders sagged. "Can we do the rest of it later?" she asked, fighting to keep her tone steady. "I guess I do need to collapse, after all."

Melina gave her arm an understanding squeeze. "Men are always convinced they know everything. We're certainly not going to admit he was right, are we?" She urged Casi into a turn. "Your room is about ten feet down this hall to the right. It has a nice big bed and a lovely bathroom all its own. Tub, not shower, so it won't be hard to keep the bandage dry."

"Sounds heavenly."

"I brought the rest of your clothes down here from the hotel ages ago. They're hanging in the closet. But I thought you might feel more comfortable in jeans and shirts just now—the kind of things we all wear out here. I bought a few things in your size. You can try them on later."

Casi made a muted sound of thanks as she was led onto a fuzzily textured shag rug. Then they were through the bedroom door and Melina was guiding her around a desk and chair, indicating the bulge of a dresser, letting her know where the bathroom was.

Moments later they had finished skimming over the rest of the small guest suite. Casi was only too happy to comply with her friend's urging to kick off her shoes. She clung to the headboard while Melina stripped back the spread. With a shudder of relief she sat, then stretched out across the bed. A cozy, satin-covered comforter was drawn up over her shoulders.

"I'm going to leave the door open." Melina's voice receded slightly. "You just holler when you wake up, okay?"

"That may be hours from now," Casi called back. "Please—just go ahead and do your own thing."

Head lolling against the pillow, she tried to quell the tremors that were rocking her body. She hadn't realized it would be this hard. The tension was unbearable. Trying to talk normally, even to Melina, seemed impossible. And around Nicholas she was a total dud. During that interminable car ride she had been constantly aware of him; his very presence disturbed her. So far she had managed to grit her teeth and pretend that what he thought of her didn't matter.

She pressed her hands to the sides of her hot cheeks, wondering what he would do if he realized how hooked on him she really was. Most likely he'd take pity on her. He might try to relieve his guilt by being nice to her for a change.

Shame at the very thought of such a thing happening stiffened her spine. She refused to be an object of his sympathy. Even if he stayed in his own house down the hill, it was too close. This simply wasn't going to work. She needed to put a continent between herself and him. Three thousand miles would have done the trick nicely. But since Dr. Harvey refused to let her go home, he'd just have to put up with her himself. It would serve him right, eavesdropping on her subconscious!

Her mind was made up. Tomorrow she'd say she wasn't feeling well, make some excuse and have Melina or Dane drive her back to the hospital.

"RIGHT ABOUT NOW you're probably sorry you came."

Casi's fingers tightened on the stem of her wineglass. Hearing her thoughts of a few hours earlier voiced in Dane's thoughtfully serious tone gave her an unreal sensation of déjà vu.

"Where are you hiding your crystal ball nowadays?" she asked her friend's husband.

"I was simply picturing how I would react in your situation," Dane explained. "Having been ruthlessly independent since the age of five, I know I would feel great resentment at having people cluck over me and help me into my clothes. It would be almost more than I could tolerate."

"Oh, Dane, it is intolerable," Casi gulped miserably. "To tell the truth, I've been trying to think up a plausible excuse to cut and run."

"For my wife's sake I am very glad you are resisting the impulse," he said, making an assumption she had no desire to live up to. "She looks happier now than I've seen her in weeks. This has been a bad time for everyone. You in particular, of course. But Melina just seemed to wilt. Even her business suffered, what with her fretting about both you and Nicholas. That's very unhealthy for her, especially now."

Casi brought her head up sharply. "With the new fall line coming out, you mean?"

Dane gave a snort of disgust. "Sometimes my mouth overwhelms my good sense! Now I've ruined her surprise."

She could hear liquid gurgling as he picked up the wine bottle and refilled her glass. He lowered his voice to make sure there was no chance of it carrying as far as the kitchen.

"No one else knows yet besides the doctor and her brother, but there was to have been a special celebration on the day following the final photography session. Our first child is due in September. She had intended to ask you to be godmother."

"How wonderful...congratulations...." Trying not to sound wistful, Casi raised her glass in a toast to the father-to-be. "You must both be so excited. But how in the world is she going to manage everything simultaneously?"

"Knowing my wife, she will find a way," Dane said, laughing. "Is there any chance you could pretend not to have heard this stupendous news until she has the opportunity to tell you herself?"

"Well, I'll try, but I've never been much of an actress." She felt for the table beside her arm and set down the glass. "I can't really say I'm surprised. Family has always meant a great deal to Melina. She used to keep pictures of everybody around, even second cousins."

"People of Portuguese blood are warm and loving and very devoted," Dane remarked. "They like to be surrounded by their kinfolk. She told me once what a source of great sorrow it was for Nicholas that his wife refused to have children. Jeanne was a newspaperwoman, you know, very wrapped up in her career."

Casi's jaw tightened. "Jeanne died four years ago. He's had plenty of time to find a new wife and father triplets by now."

"Perhaps he will, when he feels ready." She could picture Dane's accompanying shrug. "Sometimes I think he uses these causes he sponsors as a substitute for the loving family he'd prefer to devote his time to. But who knows?"

Casi didn't, that was for sure. Nicholas had been a mystery to her from the moment she arrived in California.

"As I was saying earlier, though, my main concern is Melina." Dane returned to the original topic of their conversation. "I know this is hard on you, Casi. But as a personal favor to me, would you allow her to play mother hen to you for a time?"

She kept getting put on the spot. First it was Dr. Harvey, spouting off about guilt complexes. Then Melina, pleading with her to come home for her brother's sake. Now Dane, worried about his pregnant wife. How could anyone stand up against such a gunnery team?

"Okay." She sighed. "Just think of me as the girl who can't say no to her friends."

"I'll see that you don't regret it." Almost before the promise was out of his mouth, she heard an agitated shuffle of feet. "I will regret it, however, if I don't get out there and tend the fire in the barbecue!"

The three of them dined on finger food that night: barbecued chicken, French fries and homemade rolls. The menu had obviously been planned to spare Casi embarrassment—no need to manipulate a steak knife, no roly-poly peas to balance on a fork. It was a loving gesture, typical of the Jorgensens' thoughtfulness. There had been no mention of Nicholas's joining them, for which she was extremely grateful.

"You won't mind if I go to bed early, will you?" she asked not long after the meal was concluded. "I'm afraid I've become used to keeping hospital hours."

"Whatever feels comfortable," Melina answered agreeably. "I'll come as far as the door with you. Tomorrow we'll start showing you how to find your way around the house."

Cautiously the two of them maneuvered around the living-room furniture. Once they had reached the hallway leading to the bedroom wing, Casi felt on more solid ground. "I'd like to try taking it from here," she said. "First door on the right, right?"

"Right." Melina halted, and Casi let go of her arm after locating the wall with her other hand. She made it into her bedroom without mishap. Probably her friend was still standing nervously out in the hall with her fingers crossed. But there was no time like the present to start retrieving a smidgen of her lost independence. She closed the door and began her quest for self-reliance by promptly walking into the corner of the desk.

Casi winced, rubbing her thigh. That collision was going to leave a nasty bruise. Nevertheless she was almost relieved that she had challenged the heavy desk, which had stood its ground against the impact. The chair would have toppled over with a telltale thud. She skirted it cautiously holding her hands outstretched.

Dresser, she thought. *Good show, you missed it. Bathroom door—open. Window next. Then— Damn!* She had forgotten the low nightstand.

Casi sank down on the bed, pressing one trembling hand against the other. *It will be all right soon*, she tried reassuring herself, though nothing felt all right at the moment. She just had to stop and think before she moved, find a starting point, then remember where everything was.

That afternoon Melina had gone over the room very carefully with her. There was no excuse for her having forgotten the furniture placement. But she had. That had come from being in too much of a hurry to prove herself, she supposed.

Scuffing off her low-heeled shoes, she stretched out, making sure there was enough clearance between her head and the bed's bookcase headboard. It was a temptation to drag the comforter over her and simply continue lying there, fully clothed, until morning. Sooner or later, though, she knew she would have to use the bathroom. And brush her teeth.

More than anything she longed for a hot, relaxing bath. Surely that wouldn't be too hard to manage. Nightclothes were in the nightstand, Melina had mentioned. But top drawer or bottom? Bottom, she learned after a futile search through the lingerie in the top drawer. Robe and slippers? In the closet, naturally. Casi pondered the difficulties of getting over there and back. Did she absolutely have to have them? Not really. They'd be nice, but . . . No, not really.

Snatching up the nightgown, she swung her legs over the side of the bed and forced herself to stand up before she could chicken out of any more decision making. It was easy enough to find her way into the bathroom and to recall the position of the fixtures. The towel was on the opposite wall. She draped her nightgown over it— and bashed into the hamper as she groped her way over to the edge of the tub. It had a lever-action plug, no problem to manipulate. As she reached for the taps, however, she found herself momentarily stymied again.

Was hot water on the right or the left? Casi could not remember. It was one of those automatic things; you just reached. All her life she had been turning on water without giving it a second thought. Now, just because she couldn't see an *H* or a *C*, she had become confused over which was which.

It was maddening but not vital, she soothed herself, wiggling shoulders to ease away some of the tension. The odds were fifty-fifty that she'd hit the hot one on the first try. Twisting the left faucet, she found that she had made the correct choice. Gradually she added cold water to the hot until she judged the temperature to be about right. There was a plastic container of bath salts in one corner of the tub, protected from sliding by some kind of rubber-covered fence. She dumped a handful of the crystals into the gushing foam and inhaled the heady, luxurious fragrance of gardenias.

Wrapping her hair in one of the towels, she grabbed the washcloth, and slid carefully into the tub. At last she was able to sink down in the water and enjoy the results of her trial-and-error fumbling. It had been worth the effort. But what effort!

What a day! She had been spoofing her hosts about the hospital hours. Now she found her fatigue to be very real. The worst of it was that there were still eighteen horrible days to get through before she learned whether or not this claustrophobic world of utter blackness was to be hers permanently.

Casi patted the edges of the tub, trying to remember where the soap was housed. Never, never, never, she thought, would she take anything for granted again!

4

FOR THE NEXT TWO DAYS Casi's life drifted sleepily along in a set routine. She would get up late, well after Dane's departure for his office in San Francisco. Dragging on whatever clothing came easily to hand—casual jeans, shirts and moccasins, which eliminated the need to struggle with citified attire—she would give her hair a few careless snags with the brush, then have coffee with Melina in the sunny little kitchen at the rear of the house.

Following lunch she always made some excuse to return to her room for a long nap. Then it was up again in the afternoon to sit on the patio and chat, chat, chat. She and Melina relived old times until every mutual friend and every experience they had shared had been discussed into a state of threadbareness. Often the radio was on. She could doze in the sun while giving it half an ear's attention, if that much.

During her weeks in the hospital she had lost touch with current affairs. Now Casi found that she didn't particularly care what was going on in the outside world. It had nothing to do with her. She was living from one dull moment to the next, almost as if she were in a state of suspended animation. There was nothing to do, no place to go, nothing to look forward to....

In the evening Dane would come home, kiss Melina, pour out the wine, then settle down between the two women in the living room for more conversation. Casi

hoped they weren't as bored as she was. But she knew
they must be. Already the three of them were running
out of things to say to one another. Every night she escaped to her room as soon after dinner as decency
would permit. Eating and running to give them a
chance to enjoy each other's company without her
around to intrude on their privacy.

Well, she had been ready for a good rest, Casi
thought bitterly. Unfortunately, she seemed to be more
exhausted now than when she was working, dashing
from one photo session to another, standing on her feet
all day. In her state of total lassitude energy seemed to
be a thing of the past.

On the morning following her arrival, Melina had
shown her the rest of the house. Together they had done
a walking tour of the master bedroom and the den-
office, which was situated next to the guest suite. Then
they had continued down the hall to the last door on the
right.

"This room isn't finished yet," Melina said shyly.
"The wallpaper is up, though. It's yellow, all covered
with teddy bears."

Casi drew in her breath, hoping to sound suitably
flabbergasted. "You mean a nursery?"

"Cut it out." Her friend made short work of the less
than Oscar-winning performance. "Dane has already
confessed that he spilled the beans. The two of you
ought to know better than to try to keep secrets from
me. It's wonderful news, isn't it?"

"It really is. I'm so happy for you both. You'll make
great parents."

"Well, I hope so. I'll be thirty-two this summer. That's
sort of late to be starting a family. But it isn't my fault
I didn't meet Dane until I was over the hill." Melina

laughed. "Now it's up to me to make up for lost time. I'd like to produce a whole brood to fill up these acres."

"Try for twins!" Casi joked.

"I'll mention it to the doctor." There was a little pause as they started back down the hall. "If anything, Nicholas is more excited than we are. With him for an uncle, our baby is doomed to be spoiled. He can be a most delightful person, believe it or not. And he's not terribly busy with any particular project right now. I know he would welcome some company."

"Oh, I'll bet you have neighbors just around the bend. Or he can join a bridge club," Casi answered, stonewalling the tentative suggestion. "Say, did I tell you that Grace and Tammy started a modeling school of their own in January? Can you picture those two flakes as teachers?"

"No more than I can picture any woman under ninety resisting an invitation to spend some time with my handsome brother." Melina sighed in what sounded suspiciously like exasperation. "I know you think of him as some sort of heartless monster, but he isn't that way at all. Why this terrible antagonism between the two of you?"

Casi didn't want to discuss that subject, mainly because the question was equally baffling to her. "Not everyone can like everyone," she said with a shrug. "I'll admit he is handsome, though. Doesn't he have a girlfriend of his own?"

"Not unless you count Olivia. She's far too young for him, of course, in spite of the fact that they have several interests in common," Melina said. "Being a park ranger up at Point Reyes Station, she's very much into wildlife and ecology."

"Sounds promising," Casi murmured noncommittally.

"Her grandparents keep hoping something will come of it. Soledad and Vasco have lived on the edge of our property for donkeys' years, since long before my parents were married." Earlier Melina had mentioned the woman who acted as part-time housekeeper for her and Nicholas and the man who was more or less a caretaker for Penheiro acreage. "Though she's a beautiful girl and an absolute darling, Olivia is only twenty-two. I do think an age difference of fourteen years is a little much."

"She'll be over the hill like you and me one of these days, too," Casi said lightly. "How about another cup of coffee?"

Age difference or not, Olivia sounded as if she would fit right into his life. Their backgrounds were similar, and they had interests in common. And Dane had said Nicholas wanted a family. In that respect, Olivia's age was on her side. If so inclined, she could produce half a dozen babies before reaching Casi's time of life.

IT WAS THE TELEPHONE that awakened her the third morning of her stay. Casi came to with a frightened start. She had been dreaming about noise—cable cars clanging, the wail of a siren. But it was only the phone. Beyond her door the ringing went on and on.

She struggled out of bed, grabbing for her robe, and made her way out into the hall. "Melina!" she called. "Telephone, Melina!"

Just then the peals ceased. Six steps away from her door Casi paused, her bare toes wiggling against the deep, soft pile of the carpet. The fingers of her left hand were lightly pressed against the wall; the velvety folds of her bathrobe were still clenched in her other fist. She bundled it up in her arms so as not to trip over it and turned to reverse her direction. The ringing began once more.

"Hey! Isn't anybody home?"

Casi had assumed that Melina had been out in the backyard and had run in to answer the kitchen phone. But there it went again, shrilling away relentlessly.

Aside from the strident rings the house was completely silent. Casi wavered, wondering what to do. Under ordinary circumstances she wouldn't have worried. But this was Melina's house, her phone. It was highly unusual for her not to be around to answer it. Perhaps something had happened to take her away from home unexpectedly. She might be calling to give her guest instructions.

Towing the bathrobe behind her, Casi took a few more uncertain steps toward the living room. There was an extension in there someplace. If the phone kept ringing, she ought to be able to locate it by the sound.

The wall fell away from under her fingers. She started forward, holding her hand out in front of her as she zeroed in on the direction from which the maddeningly insistent peals were issuing. In her haste and distraction she forgot everything she had been shown about the furniture's placement. She bounced off a chair and had to detour around it.

The conviction that the call had to be urgent grew with every staccato burst of sound. Stumbling onward, she caromed off another obstacle. Her knee struck something forcefully, and she heard a resounding thud. In the wake of the crash came an accompanying cacophony of noise—glass breaking, lighter objects toppling to the floor, water gurgling.

"Oh, good grief!" Casi cried aloud, dropping to her knees. She let go of the bathrobe and reached ahead of her with both hands, patting at the sodden carpet. It

was an end table she had hit, and there had been a vase
of flowers on it. Her fingers bumped the smoothly
rounded petals of a tulip. There was water everywhere, and shattered glass.... She didn't dare crawl
over the mess for fear of slashing her knees, and still the
phone kept screaming at her, sending new bursts of
alarm through her with every jangling peal.

I can't cope, she thought wildly, flinging both damp
hands up to cover her face. *I can't even cope with
something as simple as answering a telephone! How am
I going to get through the rest of my life?*

She drew in a deep, shuddering breath. In the middle of her ragged intake of air, the phone broke off in
midring, as though the caller had finally given up in
despair. That person didn't know what despair was,
Casi thought savagely as sobs started to rock her body.

There was a new flurry of sound somewhere off to her
left, hurrying footsteps followed by a muffled excla-
mation.

"What in the hell are you doing?" demanded an astonished voice.

This was the end, Casi told herself, unable to control the heaving of her chest and shoulders. To be discovered in this condition, and by him, of all people. It
was the absolute, final end!

"I don't know what I'm doing," she howled. "The
phone kept ringing and ringing, and I couldn't make
anybody hear me when I called, and I knew it must be
important—" The words jerked out a few at a time,
punctuated by shivering gasps for breath and gulping
swallows. "I am useless, useless, useless! I can't do
anything anymore!"

There were two more quick steps. Then she was being
swooped into the air and cradled in strong arms.

"It's all right, Casi. Stop it. Please stop crying," Nicholas begged in a different tone entirely. His arms tightened around her knees and shoulders as he held her closer.

"Oh, Lord, Nicholas, I was so scared!" She buried her face against his chest, dignity completely flung aside as the rasping sobs continued. Instinctively her arms twined around him. She clung to the solid, comforting presence of another human being.

His fingers spread open across her back, warming her. Flowing over his wrist and arm, her hair spun a fiery curtain as he cuddled her against the rough fabric of his shirt. "I know, I know. It's all right now. I'm here," he murmured. "You're safe. It's okay. You're not alone anymore."

Casi felt herself being carried another few feet, and then Nicholas was lowering himself onto the couch, drawing her effortlessly across his lap. She hung on tighter, letting the tears flow unchecked while he rocked her back and forth like someone doing his best with an inconsolable child. Words of comfort eddied around her as the sobs gradually diminished. His lips moved against her hair, solacing her with gentle, reassuring phrases.

It was a wonderful, dreamlike sensation. Little by little Casi's spirits floated upward from the abyss of despondency into which they had plunged. The cherishing words and soothing movements of the hand patting her shoulder seemed to be infusing hope into the terrible emptiness that had engulfed her only a short time earlier. She forgot who he was, who she was. All she knew was that she didn't want to let go. She longed for the tender moment to go on and on.

Although his warm breath was still very close, Nicholas had shifted slightly away from her. One hand rummaged in his pocket. Then linen glided across her cheek, blotting up the dampness. "Better now?" he asked.

Amazingly things were. Reluctantly, Casi drew back, tugging her right arm out from behind him and releasing his chest from the other one. Reaching out with both hands, she grasped the handkerchief and held it to her nose.

"Much better, thank you," she snuffled. "I don't know what got into me. The dam just sort of burst." Patting the air, she found his hand and returned the crumpled handkerchief. Her now-empty fingers moved forward to touch his shirt. "I got you all wet. I'm sorry."

"Feel free to do it anytime you need another blotter."

Self-consciousness flooded over her at his casual reply. Thoughts of her bedraggled appearance popped into her mind as she remembered the bathrobe, lost somewhere back between the overturned table and the broken vase. What a sight she must present to him! She was barefoot, clad only in the skimpiest of satin nightgowns, snuggled up against his chest as if . . .

An acute awareness of him flooded over her. Casi gave a little gasp and made an embarrassed effort to wiggle off his lap. The attempt was futile. One of his powerful hands still clasped her around the waist, keeping her from going anywhere.

"Really, I'm okay," she gulped, hoping to rescue a few shreds of her lost composure and convince him she could safely be turned loose. "I apologize for the cloudburst. Everything suddenly got out of hand, but I'll be fine now."

"Sure you will. And you'll feel even better after you get dressed so you can take a walk outside in the fresh air with me."

Panic struck her at the thought of trying to negotiate stairs, displaying her clumsiness to him all over again. "No, I'd rather not. Just point me toward the bedroom. I've already destroyed about fifteen minutes of your day."

"I've destroyed several weeks of your life," Nicholas reminded her quietly. "Balancing the scales will take a mighty long time. Don't you think we had better start working this through together?"

"'Together'?" As if to say it would never work, Casi shook her head. "All we've ever done together is argue."

"I'll wave a white flag if you'll fly yours. Truce?"

Casi caught her breath. He seemed to be suggesting they try friendship for a change. She was a reasonable adult, certainly. But what was the use? Any fool could figure out why he was doing this. Even so . . . She sat very still, her mind giving an instant replay of the last few things he had said to her. There hadn't been any sympathy in his voice. No sarcasm, either.

"There's nowhere for us to go but up," Nicholas pointed out after watching her think it over for a minute. "Come on, Casi. Admit that you need someone to give you a hand. I'm right here. I'd like to help, if you'll give me a chance."

If only she could see his face! All her memory could conjure up from the six-day duel of their working relationship were images of thundercloud glares, mocking scowls, arrogant orders with two rows of teeth in them. Maybe she had made a mistake. Possibly this wasn't Nicholas Penheiro's lap she was sitting on, after all. He certainly seemed to be a different man from the camera-slung fiend who had insisted she lean back and wave from the outer step of a cable car clattering up Grant Avenue!

Casi realized that it was up to her to say something. It mightn't be so bad taking a walk with him if they could do it as Nicholas and Casi, rather than perpetrator and victim. But he had to understand that there couldn't be any pity involved.

"Uh, look," she began awkwardly, "about that night. I want you to know I'm not holding it against you. You were just trying to make everything come out perfect for Melina's sake. What happened was a horrible accident, Nicholas. But it *was* an accident."

"Are you trying to say you forgive me?" he asked bitterly. "You'd have to be some sort of saint not to hate me. You aren't a saint—you're a woman. And I'm a blundering fool. The whole damned thing was my fault from beginning to end. Intentionally or not, I made it happen."

She twisted her hands nervously in her lap. "Can't you let it go? Forget it?"

"Don't you think I would if I could?"

"It isn't important any longer."

"It's vital."

Casi turned her head toward him, wishing with a kind of quiet desperation that she could read his expression.

"Vital to whom, Nicholas? You or me?"

"To both of us, dammit! To you, because you can't see. To me, because I caused that catastrophe. Now you're trying to bury the memory of it by sleeping eighteen hours a day, and I'm—I'm aware of it every waking moment."

The misery in his words tore at her heart. Hoping she might be able to give him back a little of the solace he had offered her, she raised her hand to his face. Her fingers brushed the edge of his cheek. But they had no more than encountered the damp hollow near the cor-

ner of his eye, when she felt them gripped and put firmly
aside. An instant later she was in the air again, being
carried along in a series of swinging strides.

Nicholas set her down just inside her room. "It's time
you got dressed," he said, sounding as though his jaw
were clenched with the effort of controlling his temper.
"Can I help you find anything?"

In a wordless fury Casi shook her head. "I'm not
going to get dressed. I'm going back to bed. I refuse to
have anything more to do with a walking guilt complex. You comforted me, Nicholas, when I needed
someone desperately. I tried to do the same thing for
you just now and you slapped me away. I don't need any
more rejection. Just get out of my room!"

"Oh, my God!" The words came out in a long,
shuddering breath, and then he had his arms around her
and was kissing her. "Why does everything I try to do
when I'm with you turn out all wrong?" he groaned.

He buried his lips in her hair, letting them drop in
light glides across her forehead, skirting the bandage
to sweep across her nose. His fingers curved around her
chin, tilting it up, bringing her mouth excruciatingly
close to his as his lips moved against it.

"Forgive me, sweetheart. I told you I was a blundering fool, and now I've just demonstrated it again."

The suddenness of his about-face caught Casi totally off guard. His hands had slid around her rib cage
and were clasped behind her back, drawing her up
against his chest almost before she had bitten out that
last angry word. Her upraised face had received at least
seven or eight kisses by the time she recovered from the
shock. At that point she realized that her arms were still
free. She could go ahead and pound on him or pull out
his hair.

Casi wondered if he had actually called her sweetheart. Her ears had definitely sharpened in the past few weeks. Even so, the idea that this man might use such a term of endearment when speaking to her was mindboggling. An exasperated "*Miss* Cavanaugh!" was more his usual style. But it sure had sounded like "sweetheart."

To her amazement she felt her hands creep to the top of his shoulders, then found that her fingers were linking around the back of his neck. It was bewildering, but wonderful. The crisply waving hair above his collar ruffled her skin like small, tender kisses feathering across the back of her hands. Casi let out an ecstatic sigh as rage became ardor. She exerted about a half-ounce of pressure against his nape, nudging his face down even closer to hers.

"Let's talk about it later," she whispered, feeling her lips form the words against the softness of his mouth.

She had never known a kiss so deeply passionate as the one they shared in that long moment. His lips moved across hers, nibbling around the edges of her mouth to produce a delightful sort of friction that set her pulse racing, ragtiming against her wrist. She wanted to taste him, to savor the feel of him with her tongue. Letting it swoop for a moment against the underside of his lip, she felt a scorching thrust as his responded, nudging past her teeth, trembling against hers in feverish exploration.

Bemusedly Casi slid the palms of her hands up around to his ears, exulting in their rounded shapes, which contrasted with the sweep of flowing sideburns whiskering stiffly along the sensitive lifelines traced in each palm. How many years had she longed to hold him? A lifetime, it seemed. It was bliss to be in his arms at last. The sensual brush of his hair against her skin roused a desire in her to bring him closer yet.

But Nicholas had ideas of his own. The hands criss-crossing her back slid down to her sides. They moved her torso ever so gently across his chest, encouraging her breasts to brush back and forth against him. As the kiss went on, reaching new heights of intensity every second, she could feel a throbbing ache spiraling through her body. That ever so slow, side-to-side motion of their chests was doing undreamed-of things to her libido, creating sparks, dragging a moan from the lips that were pressed against his.

Satin slithered against wool, generating an abrasive whisper, forming an erotic textural background to what she could feel happening beneath the lace-trimmed bodice of her nightgown. With every subtle movement of his hands along her sides, every sweep of her body against his, her breasts seemed to tighten, the nipples to harden and jut farther out to welcome the contact. It was a blaze-kindling torment. And the thin satin material was definitely useless as a heat shield.

Inside the filmy gown Casi began to quiver. She could feel desire rising, seeping insidiously through every corpuscle, red and white, that she called her own. And because of the manner in which their bodies were clamped together, she was being left in no doubt at all about what was happening to Nicholas's inner sensitivities.

This was insane! Only minutes before they had been snapping, almost clawing at each other. Now the claws were sheathed, and— "Oh," Casi moaned again, realizing that if this encounter didn't stop quickly it wasn't going to stop at all.

Reluctantly she dragged her head back to break the kiss. "Nicholas," she murmured against his lips.

"Talk . . . later," he groaned, reestablishing contact, taking another nibble.

Weak-willed as she was, Casi allowed herself one more tiny taste of his lips. Then she pulled away more firmly. "I think I'd better get dressed in a hurry," she forced herself to say. "Really, this isn't the time or the place."

"Sure about that?"

A tremor rocked her as she remembered that beautifully soft mattress a few feet away on the other side of the room. "A few minutes ago you were implying that I spent too much time in bed."

"I said you were *sleeping* eighteen hours a day. Not—"

"Not . . . a very good idea." Casi sighed, resisting the impulse to drag him between the sheets.

"You're probably right," Nicholas relented. "Another thirty seconds and that truce of ours would be history. I'd be groveling in unconditional surrender."

At her rib cage his fingers tightened. He inched her one more time across the front of him. Shuddering, he stepped back a pace. "You'd better break speed records getting your clothes on. Meanwhile I'll see what I can do about taking care of the debris in the living room. With any luck there'll be some cold water left in the bottom of the vase that I can pour over myself."

A secret smile touched her lips as she sensed the motion of his body brushing past her. Relatively confident by now about the furniture arrangement in her room, she walked toward the dresser in search of something to wear. But Nicholas delayed her when he paused on the threshold.

"Uh, Casi?"

"Yes, Nicholas?"

"You're a fantastic therapist."

"Thanks." Her smile widened. "Wait till you get my bill!"

She heard the door close as she tugged open a drawer. A woodsy scent of cedar emanated from the bureau. Casi dragged out jeans and a sweatshirt, feeling for the first time in a long while that she had something to look forward to. She had every intention of collecting on that threatened invoice. Nicholas could repay her in kisses and hugs and—

"Oh, my goodness," she muttered to herself. "I wonder if there's enough water left in that vase to put out *two* fires."

The way things had been heading they would have created a sensational conflagration. But blazes of that nature were meant to be started and quenched in total privacy. She'd had no intention of risking the chance that Melina might come home and find her houseguest in bed with her big brother.

As the latch clicked behind her, Casi paused on the porch to inhale appreciatively. There was a pure snap to the air so unlike the crazy, mixed-up city goo she was accustomed to breathing. On impulse she stuck out her tongue.

"If you're making faces at someone, there's nobody here except me," Nicholas said. "Quarter turn to your left."

"I'm trying to decide if I can taste salt. See what you think."

There was a brief pause. She smiled, picturing him slurping at the air.

"Little pepper, wisp of cinnamon. Not quite enough salt," he decided. "Let's go right down to the shoreline and try it again. Which would you prefer, hand or arm?"

"Arm, please." Casi reached toward the elbow crooked obligingly in her direction. "I may take up the other option later. But I've already had my catastrophe for the day, and I don't hanker for any more bruises."

She held on tightly with her left hand, letting the right one hang free. By regulating the swing of her foot, she discovered that going down stairs could be much easier than ascending. It was just a matter of letting her sole drop until it touched bottom.

"Very good," Nicholas complimented her. His arm tightened, hugging her hand against his side.

"Gravel path, forty feet," Casi recalled. "What next?"

"Then comes the road and across from it a chunk of wilderness. Brambly undergrowth, sea oats and tall purple clusters of wild lupin. We're going to turn left before we get that far. Halfway between this house and my own is a well-trodden path that will lead us down to the beach."

Casi could feel the bangs riffling against her forehead as she and Nicholas swung along, side by side, their long strides evenly matched. It felt marvelous to be outside again, walking, instead of dozing in the house. She wondered if she could really have endured that inactivity for three full weeks, or whether her body would have rebelled, even without Nicholas's intervention.

He snapped his fingers in sudden recollection. "I never did tell you the reason I walked in and found you having it out with the living room," he exclaimed. "Early this morning Melina got a call from her assistant. Some problem having to do with the design studio had arisen. There was no choice but for her to make a quick trip into the city. She phoned to ask if I could come over and keep you company until she got home.

I was out riding. Soledad took the message and passed it on to me—an hour late, I'm sorry to say."

"Oh," Casi murmured. "Well, I'm glad you arrived in time to close the spillway gates. I hope the carpet is dry when she gets home."

The house would have been empty for hours, she thought. There really hadn't been any reason to get dressed in such a hurry, after all.

Suddenly she had the impression that he was peering closely at her.

"We haven't been outside long enough for you to get a sunburn. Casi, are you blushing?"

"Why would I do a thing like that?"

"I can't think of any reason." He didn't sound quite satisfied.

"Then I guess it must be the sun," Casi said blandly.

Nicholas tugged his arm forward, moving her on, but he kept turning his head in her direction as they walked. She really was a terrible liar, he thought. No finesse at all. That sudden wash of color across her cheeks had deepened even more. Whatever she was keeping to herself undoubtedly concerned him. Something to do with that scene in the bedroom, maybe.

He tightened his jaw, shuddering at the recollection of how close he had come to completely alienating Casi. And all because he'd been afraid she might discover that his eyes were wet, too. He couldn't remember how many years had passed since he'd been moved to tears.

A "walking guilt complex," she had called him. That wasn't far from the truth. Every time he looked at that bandage his heart wanted to break. And yet she had responded to him with an ardor that had sent his senses reeling. The thought of what the nearness of her body and the warm, tender pressure of her lips had done to his temperature still prompted tremors inside him. The difficulty of suppressing his desire for her had left his throat parched, a tight, painful ache binding his chest. Having to walk this close to her and still keep his hands to himself was torture.

He shot another sideways glance at her. That beautiful oval face was still suspiciously pink. She didn't like him. He knew that, of course. But she hadn't minded kissing him. Not a bit. If he could just keep from rushing her, manage to do something right for a change....

Nicholas sighed. Maybe it wasn't too late. The odds were a million to one against her taking him on any terms now, but as long as that one chance remained alive... Strolling along, he speculated on her remark about the invoice. Whatever the cost of that therapy, he would pay it gladly.

Observing that the path was steep and winding and that roots stuck out in places to snare an unwary foot, he insisted on carrying her down the embankment. Casi was only too happy to be lifted into his arms once again. Contentedly she leaned her head on his shoulder and wrapped one arm loosely around his neck while his jogging gait carried them downhill. His massive strength inspired supreme confidence, and she loved the way his back felt against her hand. The warmth of him penetrated even his thick shirt; the sinewy muscles rippled in easy rhythm under her fingertips.

Casi wondered what had happened to them all of a sudden. One minute they were yelling at each other and the next they were locked in a passionate embrace. What a tension reliever those kisses had been! One kind of tension, at least. The other kind was still whispering through her body, making it awfully, awfully hard to keep her lips to herself. It didn't seem possible that the man in whose arms she now rested was the photographer she had hoped would fall overboard.

Casi crossed her fingers that there was nothing seriously wrong at the design studio. Nevertheless she couldn't help hoping that a few more business complications would arise, spurring Melina into making daily trips to the city.

Even from the road the sound of the sea had been clearly audible. As they continued the descent, the constant ebb and flow of the surf became even more pronounced. The surging foam seemed to be murmuring enticingly to them. "Come ahead," it beckoned. "Join with me."

"Can we go wading?" she asked.

"We certainly cannot. This far north the Pacific is like liquid ice in March," Nicholas answered firmly. "Do you want blue toes to match your livid bruises?"

"At least I'd be color coordinated!"

It was quite a long hike to the bottom, but Nicholas wasn't even winded when at last he set her down. Casi's moccasins scrunched against the sand. For a few steps she shuffled deliberately, enjoying the gritty scrape of it beneath her feet. She let go of Nicholas's arm and tucked her fingers inside his hand.

"It sounds beautiful," she said, gesturing toward the sighing ocean. "And between the sun on my face and the sand underfoot, it feels simply glorious. Tell me how it looks."

Nicholas gave the request his serious consideration. "This part of the coast has sort of a raw beauty," he said after a minute. "The ocean dominates everything with its awesome power, but the cliffs continue to resist its force. The only litter is that which nature herself provides—fat coils of washed-up seaweed in a few places, here and there chipped shells scoured clean by the wave action."

Impulsively he turned to her. "Casi, I—what can I say? I'd give anything in the world if you could see it yourself."

"I hope I will someday." Her fingers tightened over his, telling him silently not to care so much. "Today I'm content to look at it through your eyes."

Clenching the fist she wasn't holding, Nicholas remembered that devastating storm of tears he had interrupted. He had brought her to the depths of despair. Yet she was willing, for now, to let him be her eyes. It was all he could do to resist enfolding her within the circle of his arms once again. This was the woman he wanted. The one who had been designed by heaven or fate for the express purpose of sharing his life. And he had nearly killed her before he could bring himself to admit the truth.

Swallowing the lump of raw emotion clogging his throat, he made an effort to continue making this vista he loved so dearly come alive for her.

"Behind us is a double line of footsteps, one set much deeper than the other. Are you aware that you're far too slender? This morning I had the impression I was holding a double handful of satin-sheathed cotton candy."

He felt her shiver and paused to zip the closing of her jacket right up under her chin. "Up here the sand is a golden crescent the color of lightly toasted bread," he went on, before she could protest that she wasn't really chilly. "A little farther on down, the tide is scalloping big, dark circles across it. Every time the water pulls back it leaves little flecks of foam behind. They cling for a time, and then, as they dry up, the breeze puffs them away. The wet pebbles tumble a few inches toward the ocean with every sweep of the tide. They're very shiny. The light is striking this side of them, making them glisten like precious stones."

Casi's other hand crossed over. For a brief moment she caressed his fingers with all ten of hers. "That's very beautiful, Nicholas. I really can see it. There's a lot of green in the ocean, isn't there, as well as blue? And the foam bubbling on top looks like meringue that has separated on top of a pie."

The caw of a seabird echoed raucously from not far away. Overhead, Casi heard wings flap as other gulls were drawn by the cry to quarrel over the tidbit their companion had found.

"He made the mistake of boasting too loudly," Nicholas said with a chuckle. "Now he must fight off the predators for possession of what he snatched out of the ocean. He's ruffling his feathers most indignantly at them, shaking his beak back and forth, as if to tell them to go do their own scavenging."

They walked on, hearing the flock complain and take wing at their approach. Scuffing in the sand, Nicholas bent down for an instant. "Here is something you can look at for yourself," he said, tucking a small object into her palm. He released her other hand to allow her to pay full attention to his prize. "Tell me what your mind perceives about what you are holding, Casi."

"It's a shell. Abalone, but much smaller than the ones I've seen at Fisherman's Wharf," she mused aloud, rubbing her fingers along the crusty underside of it. "About ten little bumps curve around from top to bottom. Some of the holes are open, but the upper ones are still closed. They'd have probably all expanded if the poor thing had survived long enough to grow up. There's a whorled ridge from the top extending halfway around the left side, and in the center it's smooth, with delicate arching lines traced into it. I think this side must be shiny."

An odd, husky note characterized Nicholas's voice. "Silver shiny, like a new dime. Not only that, but iridescent where the sun strikes it, throwing out reflections of red and green. As if a tiny rainbow had toppled out of the sky and trickled onto the surface."

Casi's face was very still for a time. After a moment she tucked the baby abalone carefully into the pocket of her jacket and reached for his hand again. "Your books always made me want to cry, too," she said quietly. "You talk and write about nature as though your soul is having a love affair with it."

They walked on in silence.

About a quarter mile farther up the beach Nicholas called a halt, decreeing that it was time for a rest. Along that area the sand was studded with driftwood sunning itself, and he didn't want to risk having her trip and fall. Her self-confidence had come a long way today; he intended to go on nurturing it very carefully. He located a massive bleached log for them to lean back against.

"It must have been lovely growing up here," Casi remarked. "This property has been in your family for a long time, hasn't it?"

"Nearly a century. When my grandfather was fifteen he signed on to work his way across the ocean aboard a merchant vessel. After he arrived in San Francisco he labored as a fisherman in the daytime and as a waiter at night," Nicholas said. "He saved every penny he could get his hands on to buy this acreage. Then he kept right on working and scrimping until he was able to afford a trip back to Portugal. His goal was to marry the girl he had left behind and bring her back here to live with him. He said there was no one in America as beautiful as his Luisita."

"She waited for him all that time?"

"Luisita was a one-man woman," he said simply. "And for my grandfather, she was the only woman alive. They were both thirty-five by the time they were reunited, but neither of them ever regretted the decision to wait until they could have each other."

"Twenty years' devotion!"

"And fifty-seven afterward. My father was the eldest of their four children. Because of wars and what not, he didn't marry until he was past forty, so there was only Melina and I to grow up here instead of the larger family they might have had. But my cousins and their parents used to come back frequently for family get-togethers."

"I'd like to have been part of a tribe like that."

Idly Nicholas tossed a small piece of driftwood from hand to hand. "You know I'm to be an uncle in the fall. It's nice to think that there will be another young family growing up here in years to come."

"Yes. I've been asked to be godmother."

Casi sensed that this was an extremely delicate subject. Remembering her conversation with Dane a few evenings before, she guessed that Nicholas's thoughts were centered on the family he himself had been denied.

Before her life had been put on hold by the accident, settling down to domestic life had been one of her own dreams. She recalled how seriously she had contemplated chucking modeling in favor of choosing a husband and getting on with the process of filling up a nursery herself while there was still time. Over the years she had turned down any number of proposals while she waited for the right man to come along. But he never had. Recently the idea of making a selection from among the group of eligible bachelors who were still tagging along in her wake had become increasingly more attractive. She really couldn't drag her feet much longer in the hope that the glint of shining armor would show up on the horizon.

If, when the bandages came off her eyes, the odds turned out in her favor, she'd go ahead and settle on someone pretty soon. But making that decision was going to be much harder now. It was just her luck to find someone who could make her pulse jump by just a word or a touch and have him be the one unattached male of her acquaintance who didn't care for her at all.

Some women were lucky enough to meet and marry their one true love and some weren't, she thought wistfully. Her mother had, and so had Melina. And faithful Luisita. That really must have been a grand passion for her to go on patiently refusing all other suitors until she was able to wed the one man she wanted.

"What are you thinking about?" Nicholas asked.

Casi trailed her fingers in the sun-kissed sand. "Oh, nothing and everything. Families and lifetime devotions, that sort of thing. Like Luisita, my mother was a one-man woman, although she and my dad didn't have very many years together. He was a helicopter pilot who was killed when I was small. His name was Casey. She named me after him and just changed the spelling to a more feminine form."

"Your mother is no longer living?"

"No. She got very sick about three years ago. There was a mix-up in prescriptions at the pharmacy. The wrong medicine was enough to—to end it."

"She remained a widow all that time?"

"Some people aren't willing to settle for second best," Casi said, hoping she wasn't going to be among that forlorn group. "It wasn't easy for her, raising me all by herself, but she managed the job just fine. I still miss her a lot."

Nicholas tossed away the driftwood and lay his hand over hers. "So your family is gone. Is there anybody else back in New York?"

"Swarms of them. All tied for second best." She answered his meaning rather than his words.

"Nothing in particular binds you to the East Coast, then?"

"It's where I live and work. But of course—" Casi stopped herself just in time. He had enough on his conscience to bedevil him already. What purpose would it serve to punish him with the additional revelation that now she would need to find a new line of work? "Of course I've got tons of friends there," she substituted feebly.

The hand holding hers stiffened. "The other morning in the car you said you didn't approve of playing games with the language just to salve someone's feelings," he reminded her. "Why don't you finish what you started to say?"

Casi wished she were less sensitive to the changes in his tone, less sensitive to him altogether. Where Nicholas was concerned, her emotions were one long, bumpy knot of worry beads. Half the time this man made her want to poke him in the nose. Half the time he made her want to cry over him and find a way to heal whatever was troubling him; kiss the spot and make it well. Half the time she wanted to climb back into his lap and kiss him for another reason entirely.

No third-grade teacher would ever accept that sort of arithmetic. What it came down to was that he was an extremely complex person who mixed her up as much as he stirred her up. The physical attraction she felt for him was positively awesome. But she forced herself to keep it rigidly in check, miserably aware that he was here with her now for all the wrong reasons.

Casi took a deep, unsteady breath. "Look, Nicholas, there are exceptions to every rule. Man-woman relationships aren't the easiest thing in the world to deal with. So far ours has been as steep and curvy and full of pitfalls as that slippery route up to Coit Tower. For some reason I never understood, we started off all wrong and nearly wound up enemies. Then, because of the accident, you figured you owed me something. This morning...this morning we discovered a few more things about each other. I was given an insight of how kind and gentle you can be, and... and you took a step toward letting someone hug you back."

He brought her fingers up to his lips. "I think that what you're trying to say is, 'Let's not hurt each other anymore.'"

Casi turned her pale, oval face toward him. "Do you think that's possible? To throw out the past like Melina's broken vase and start again? To take this in easy stages, but keep it moving forward instead of back?"

"I'd like that very much," he said huskily. "Would you?"

"I can't think of anything nicer." Casi struggled to her feet. "Nicholas, this gruesome bandage is getting soggy again. Shall we try jogging back, to give it a chance to dry out in the wind?"

5

"YOU MEAN THEY'RE GOING on strike?" Casi asked in a horrified tone. "How can they do that to you? You have a contract with the garment workers' union, don't you?"

"Of course I've got a contract! But the shop steward figures he has me over a barrel because of the tightness of the delivery schedule. Dozens of orders could be canceled if we don't get the clothing into the stores by late August, and he knows it. He's urging the seamstresses to make new demands, agitate for more fringe benefits. . . . I don't know what to do!" Melina sounded as if she were about ready to burst into tears.

"The first thing you're going to do is calm down," Dane insisted firmly. "No group of dresses is worth a nervous breakdown. Or the risk of injuring your health and that of the baby. Did you call your attorney?"

"Yes. And the union called their attorney. Both men spent the afternoon sharpening their ripostes. They certainly didn't accomplish much else," Melina grumbled. "Meanwhile the workers are sitting around yawning on their needles."

Casi slumped back in her chair while the Jorgensens continued to talk it out. The entire household had been in a turmoil since Melina arrived home with the appalling news that afternoon. At least Nicholas's angry rumbles weren't being added to this conversation. He had taken off as soon as the first car—Dane's—had appeared in the driveway, saying he had an errand to do. She couldn't help resenting the speed with which he had vanished. That hasty departure had given the distinct impression that he was already tired of his baby-sitting chores.

Earnestly hoping that her earlier accident hadn't left a stain on the carpet and that it would be days before the absence of the vase was noticed—minor things had been known to provide the proverbial last straw—she tried to think whether there was anything she could do to ease this situation. But even when sighted, sewing hadn't been one of her skills. To the best of her knowledge she had never come face-to-face with an attorney, and she wouldn't have known a shop steward from a textile spinner.

The incipient wildcat strike was, of course, the reason for Melina's early dash into the city that morning. Bad news had continued to catch up with the dress designer as she journeyed from home to studio to garment plant to law offices. Obviously the demanding phone summons that had catapulted Casi into a new relationship with Nicholas was merely part of that whole nerve-wracking chain of events.

With a pang Casi remembered her wish as she was being carried down the steep embankment to the shoreline in Nicholas's arms. It had been a foolish thing, just one of those hopeful spurts of imagination, which argued that if Melina was called upon to make frequent trips into San Francisco, the two of them would have no alternative but to entertain each other. Now the recollection made her feel oddly culpable, just as her harmless fantasy about the shark had provoked such intense self-recriminations that she had babbled about it under sedation. She was beginning to understand what guilt complexes were all about.

For the ninth time in an hour the phone shrilled. "I'll get it," Dane growled, shoving back his chair. His footsteps cracked an angry tattoo across the floor.

Casi grabbed the opportunity for a private word with Melina. "While all this is going on, you're not to be worrying about me," she insisted. "Between morning sickness and this new dilemma, you have enough to deal with. I can cope. If necessary, we'll string a lifeline from bedroom to kitchen. I want your promise that you won't let the fact that I'm here keep you from concentrating on your business."

Melina's rings were clicking again, making agitated noises as her hands twisted together. "I did feel dreadful going off and leaving you without a word. But you needed your rest, and I knew Soledad would give Nicholas the message right away. Uh, were there any problems?"

"A few," Casi admitted cautiously. "After that we got along pretty well, considering Nicholas's touchy temperament and my waspish disposition. We spent several hours on the beach, telling each other stories about our childhood."

"I'm so relieved. It sounds as if you've made a good start. Just be firm with him, Casi. Sometimes my brother is inclined to be rather...pushy. But if you can, be kind, too. He hasn't been very happy these past few years."

"Is there anything at all I can do to help you through this situation at work?" Casi asked, trying to avoid any further discussion of Nicholas. "With a big-enough pad of paper I could sit by the phone and scrawl down messages."

"Thanks, but I have a very capable secretary. What I really need right now is a combination Perry Mason and old-time strike breaker." Melina's giggle sounded a trifle hysterical. "If all else fails, I'll give in to them. I can't afford to let this continue for long. Every cent I have is tied up in this venture, as well as a great deal of Dane's savings and some money I borrowed from Nicholas."

"Fortunately a thrifty drop of Scottish blood crept in to mingle with the feckless Irish in my background," Casi remarked, trying to sound casual. "The result being a fairly healthy bank account from all those plum modeling assignments. If you should find yourself with your back against the wall and the firing squad starts lining up . . ."

"That's the best offer I've had all day by a very wide margin," Melina said tremulously. "Thanks. I'm sure a loan won't be necessary, but I'll keep it in mind."

As on the previous morning Casi awoke to noise. This time, however, it was a cheery whistle emanating from the kitchen. She crossed the room and opened her door.

"Who have I got for company?" she called.

"The blundering fool," Nicholas's voice trailed back to her. "Hurry up and get decent. Breakfast is almost ready, and then I've got something to show you."

Casi could feel a smile quirking her lips. "Go ahead and start without me. I don't eat breakfast."

"Under the Penheiro regime you do. Move it!" There was a threatening pause. Then his voice approached as far as the living room. "Unless you'd rather I came in and gave you a hand . . . or two?"

"That's all right, Nicholas. I think I can manage." Casi quickly closed the door and headed for the cedar-lined bureau. "Pushy" was certainly the word to describe him, all right! Tugging denim and cotton over lace, she let the smile widen. He would have come in, too. And there would have gone the "easy stages" aspect of the new man-woman relationship they were trying to build. She wasn't anywhere near confident enough about her feelings toward him to let that happen yet.

"Pancakes?" she asked incredulously a few minutes later. "*And* eggs? Nicholas, you're not feeding threshers!"

He pulled out a chair, sat down beside her and placed a fork firmly in her right hand. "Nope. Just a houseguest made out of cotton candy. Come on, Casi. Take a few bites. Otherwise I'll think you're casting slurs on my cooking. I don't need any more rejection!"

She choked, hearing her words of the previous morning come back to haunt her. She'd better manage the fork by herself, Casi realized. One touch of that strong hand across hers had been enough to produce shivers. Maybe it was a good idea to keep up her strength.

When she had eaten as much as she possibly could, urged on by his gentle prodding, she set down her fork with finality. "Did I hear you say you had something to show me?"

Nicholas started removing plates from the table. "Yeah. I went and got them last night as soon as Dane came home. I was afraid the stores would close before I could make it into town. Otherwise I wouldn't have taken off so fast."

Relief shot through her system, unraveling the knot of uncertainty that had nagged at her last evening. "Oh. I thought that maybe—"

"Maybe I'd had enough of you for one day? No way, Casi." His voice had an odd timbre to it. She could feel a hand glide across the back of her hair and then remove itself quickly, as though it were afraid it might get into trouble if it stayed there very long. He crossed the room and returned almost immediately. She heard two small plunks as objects were set atop the wooden surface.

"These mightn't even be necessary, since I intend spending a great deal of time with you from now on. But I wanted to make very sure you didn't get out of touch with the world again," Nicholas said. "I've got a couple of two-way radios here. Sophisticated walkie-talkies, really. I'm going to teach you to use yours, so all you'll have to do is holler if you need me and I'm not around."

A moment later a small, plastic-cased rectangle was being inserted between her hands. "Feel the lever on the side?"

"Yes," Casi murmured, overcome by this evidence of thoughtfulness. Her fingers moved across the surface of the instrument, taking note of the short antenna and the circular grating on the front.

"Turn it, then hold the screen close to your mouth. Say a few words and listen to what happens."

She obeyed and heard an echo of her voice from the second radio on the table. "When the lever isn't turned it stays on Receive?" she asked. "You can talk back to me?"

"That's the way it works," Nicholas said. "Whenever I'm not with you I want you to keep it within reach. Mine will be either hung from a belt around my waist or on the nightstand by my bed. If you need me or—or just get lonesome or frightened at night, pick it up. I'll hear you."

"My gosh." Casi tried not to let the emotion she was feeling tremble into her voice. "That's great. My own portable security blanket."

"It's a two-way transmitter, remember." Nicholas gave a rather shaky laugh. "Don't be surprised if you hear a few sweet nothings whispered into your ear now and then."

Casi wondered how one answered airborne sweet nothings. She bit her lip. "Thank you."

He got up hastily. "Want to give it a trial run? These are good for up to a mile. I'm going to take mine outside."

Their conversation, as they practiced from various ranges, wouldn't have raised any eyebrows even if someone had been listening in. Nevertheless, that one-mile limit tickled Casi. Other small communicators, she knew, were much more powerful. It was nice to know that whatever might be murmured over the airwaves wouldn't be intercepted by the avid ears of some enthusiastic ham operator.

Eventually Nicholas came back inside, satisfied with the results of the test. "I'll take mine along, but you leave yours here. You won't be needing it the rest of the day," he said.

"Are we going to the beach again?"

"Not right now." He took her hand, urging her out of the chair. "I want you to come over to my house and meet Soledad."

Casi stiffened. "I'm—I'm not very comfortable around strangers just now, Nicholas."

He continued to hoist her up. "Soledad is family. She and Vasco are almost like my own grandparents. You're going to love her." He paused, watching her hesitate. "Don't you like the idea of a chaperon? You'll be a lot safer that way," he teased.

Casi made an effort to overcome her reluctance. She wasn't a side-show freak, after all, just a person who was walking around in the dark at the moment. And if she didn't want a chaperon . . . She reached for his elbow. "When you put it in those terms, I guess I don't dare refuse."

Nicholas paused to strap the radio around his waist. "Start counting steps, Casi. It's important that you learn to find your way to the front door with confidence, just in case you ever smell smoke or something. Okay?"

"Okay." She set her mind to this next task, remembering how confused she had become the day before when trying to locate the telephone. For the sake of fire safety alone, it was worth making this effort. More than that, though, she wanted to please him by becoming a quick learner.

Strolling along the road beside him, Casi thrust aside the fear of meeting someone who had not yet been exposed to her masked appearance. Nicholas was taking her to his house, his old childhood home. It gave her an achingly sweet feeling of intimacy with him, as though in a small way she were being included as part of his family.

There had been a snapshot of the house in one of Melina's numerous photo albums. It was a long, low building, thick-walled for insulation against the heat and dampness, Casi remembered. The adobe sides were painted white, the trim a fresh charcoal. Black wrought iron spiraled decoratively around windows, and topping the ranch-style structure was a glistening red tile roof.

That old picture had shown a happy family group clustered along the arched supports of the wide veranda. It wasn't a very good shot, since shade had intruded to dim their likenesses, but it emphasized the fact that the long porch provided a cool retreat against the glare of the afternoon sun. Green plants, including the plaited donkey tail that Luisita had brought from Portugal, hung in overflowing baskets in each of the three front arches.

Now, cutting catercorner across the lawn, her fingers clamped tightly around Nicholas's powerful arm, Casi felt trailing greenery brush lightly against her hair as the veranda's serene atmosphere engulfed her. They entered the house and stepped onto cool parquet flooring. The door, which closed behind them, fell to with the massive-sounding thud of solid oak.

Her first impression was one of tranquillity. The second, following hard on the first, was that the house smelled absolutely delicious.

Casi took a deep breath; the air was redolent with the savory fragrance of yeast. "Is that what I think I smell?" she asked incredulously.

"Bread baking? One of Soledad's specialties," Nicholas informed her. "You're going to have a couple of thick slabs of it with your lunch, lavishly spread with butter and homemade jam."

"On top of those pancakes? You really don't give a darn about my figure, do you?"

"Oh, but I do," he insisted. "The next time I take you in my arms I want something of substance to hold."

Casi caught her breath. She hadn't forgotten the intensity of their kisses, or the way her body had responded to his nearness. Even in that brief embrace yesterday she had experienced a surge of desire, a thrill of bliss that had thoroughly shaken her. Now Nicholas was calmly informing her that a second encounter was on his mind.

"What's the matter?" he said with a laugh. "No springing to the defense of low-calorie salads?"

"I'm very fond of salad," she said snippily. "That was the first time a man's intentions toward me were ever stated in terms of how fast I gained weight. I was only wondering whether you meant that remark as a threat or a promise." Casi's voice was demure, her racing pulse anything but.

His fingers curled more tightly about hers. "Consider it a vow," he said quietly. "When the time comes, you'll enjoy being in my arms. You won't want to leave them so quickly again."

He'd given her fair warning, Nicholas thought. If she wanted to run, he couldn't stop her. But she could stop him. All she had to do was say no again. Would she?

Casi's knees were wobbling. She forced the betraying limbs to move her resolutely along beside this man who spoke so openly about making love to her. He was right, she decided. She would never be able to back away a second time. Just thinking about the fever he had aroused in her left her too light-headed to respond. "When the time comes," he had said. Would it be long?

She didn't even remember crossing the rest of the house. It wasn't until rigid squares of tile replaced carpet underfoot and she heard a whoop of greeting that she snapped out of her daze. Soledad was a billowy lady, judging from the ample girth that enfolded Casi the moment Nicholas introduced her. The housekeeper ignored the bandage and began making motherly sounds immediately.

"Ai, so tall and beautiful," she exclaimed. "But thin, like my granddaughter. I keep telling Olivia she'll never get a good man until she puts some meat on her bones. He'll think she doesn't know how to cook!"

So Olivia was slender, as well as twenty-two and gorgeous, Casi thought ruefully. That was a hard combination to fault.

"Well, it's clear that Vasco, at least, is a contented husband." She forced herself to smile, inhaling once again. "The bread smells wonderful. I can't wait to taste it."

"Don't worry. She's almost as anxious to feed you as I am," Nicholas said. "I want you to get acquainted with this room, because we'll be spending a lot of time in it."

It was one of those huge, old-fashioned kitchens built long before the modern trend toward compactness, Casi realized as they embarked on a leisurely tour. The stone hearth built into one wall was large enough to accommodate half a cow when the occasion called for it. The solid wooden table would easily seat twelve. Along a sunny, plant-filled window was a comfortable, slip-covered old sofa, just right for lounging on after a giant-sized meal. In another corner stood an antique wooden rocking chair. It was unquestionably a family room.

"I'm simply green with envy," she exclaimed. "Nicholas, what a wonderful childhood you and Melina must have had here!"

"We did. I only wish—"

He didn't finish the sentence. *He's worse than me, keeping things bottled up inside,* she thought. "What do you wish, Nicholas?" she asked gently.

But he wouldn't talk about it. "I had an uncle who used to say that if wishes were horses, beggars would ride." He dropped the subject.

The bread had come out of the oven. Not content to let it cool on the rack, Nicholas took a knife out of the drawer and hacked off a hot slice for Casi, as well as one for himself. Soledad caught him in the act.

"Since you were a two-year-old I have been telling you to let the bread rest a bit before you start eating," she scolded.

Casi suspected that Soledad secretly would have been disappointed if Nicholas hadn't shown an impatience to taste the thick, yeasty loaf. Taking a mouthful herself, she understood his reluctance to wait.

"Oh, that's wonderful! Soledad, could I have just one more crumb?" she begged when the remains of the first slice had been devoured.

"Now I have two of you to contend with, one as bad as the other. Shoo! Out of the kitchen," she ordered, flapping her apron at them. "In one hour you will have your lunch, not before."

"That's what is known as getting our walking papers," Nicholas said indulgently. "Come on, Casi. There's something I want you to see, anyway."

He had used the word quite naturally, she realized, and remembered Melina's horror only a few days before when she slipped and said, "Look—" Thank heaven Casi had put her foot down and insisted that people go ahead and talk, rather than juggling words to spare her feelings! Besides, Nicholas really did expect her to "see" things, as he had demonstrated quite vividly yesterday on the beach. Several times after that first incident with the abalone shell, he had indicated that she was to use her fingers to make up for some of the things her eyes were missing.

With her hand in his, she followed along as he led her out the patio door, down a step and across a wooden deck. Even before reaching the grass, a heady aroma wafted toward her, the perfumed fragrance of a medley of spring flowers blooming close by.

Casi inhaled the mingled potpourri. "This must be a glorious sight," she said pensively, regretting that she was missing what must be a riot of color. "Stock and sweet peas, hyacinth and violets. I know them all."

"From florist shops or flower stands on street corners? In New York they would be luxuries. Here the blooms are part of our lives," Nicholas said. "This is my mother's flower garden. She never planted another seed after our father died, but with Vasco's help Melina and I try to keep it up the way she always laid it out."

His family seemed to be riddled with one-man women, and Casi had to wonder if all the Penheiro men were so dedicated to their spouses, as well. In spite of Jeanne's refusal to bear his children, it was possible Nicholas was still pining for her. Being a man with normal needs, he might steal a kiss or more occasionally, but allowing himself to love again was quite another thing. Perhaps that was what he had been wishing about in the kitchen—that his wife were still alive and there with him to share that marvelous room with all its family memories.

The idea provoked a deep well of sadness within her, for herself as well as for him. She was more than half in love with Nicholas already. Every touch of his hand seemed to promise a growing affection between the two of them. But if it developed into something more than friendship, she didn't think she could bear to live with the knowledge that she would always be second best as far as he was concerned.

If only he would talk about the things that really mattered she might have a better chance to judge what the future might bring. Every step she took nowadays—emotionally as well as physically—was a venture into the unknown. With only a little more encouragement she would be able to open her heart to him fully and for all time. But she didn't want that vital organ to emerge from this encounter with as many bruises as her body had already sustained.

Casi shook her head to clear it. Only yesterday they had promised each other to move forward, not back. And here in her own thoughts she was already erecting fences. Fences . . .

"Nicholas, where's Gulliver?" she asked, halting suddenly. "I haven't heard a single bark since we drove up here Monday morning."

He squeezed her hand reassuringly. "At the moment he is in residence with Vasco and Soledad. As you heard, he is an excitable dog with an incurable tendency to fling himself into people's arms. I couldn't take a chance on him knocking you off your feet. All he would do is lick your face, but you looked pretty frightened when he rushed up to the car."

"Dogs have always been my nemesis," she confessed. "When I was about seven I was attacked by a huge beast running loose in Central Park. His teeth were bared and he was slobbering—" She shuddered convulsively. "Fortunately a policeman dragged him off me in time, but every once in a while I still wake up at night dreaming that he's leaping at my throat. To this day I've never been able to so much as look at a poodle without flinching."

Nicholas urged her to continue across the yard. "That was a once-in-a-lifetime misfortune, Casi. You can't go through life being afraid of things. I won't allow it."

Casi found his possessive tone slightly irritating. "You can't change everything about me," she said shortly. "Some fears are like your beggars' wishes. Unanswerable."

"But others can be dissolved," Nicholas replied. "In the next two weeks we might make some progress toward doing that."

He, too, was willing to look forward rather than back, Casi realized. Maybe if she just relaxed and let things run their course without worrying about bruises . . . For now it was enough to know that he intended to spend the next two weeks at her side. Relaxing the tense grip the thought of dogs had provoked, she sighed in contentment and walked on.

After crossing a rough patch of open ground where the sun had warmed her hair, Casi found herself stepping into shadows again. She heard the rusty creak of an old wooden door being swung open and then found her feet sloughing across a resilient surface. Unlike grass or carpet, this new crackling texture seemed almost to flow beneath her feet.

"Is that hay down there?"

"Yes." Nicholas laughed. "How did you know?"

"The way it slithered around, I guess. Besides, I've spent a lot of time in livery stables. This smells like a place for animals. Or it used to be," she added, wrinkling her nose. "The straw and manure—everything's old and weathered. You don't keep horses here anymore?"

"Casi, I'm impressed!" He sounded proud of her. "You're right. This old barn hasn't been used much recently. Nowadays I keep my horse up at Vasco's stable along with Olivia's because I'm away so much."

"Do the two of you go riding often?" That darned girl's name had been popping up too often for comfort, Casi thought. A long-dead Jeanne was one thing, but Olivia was part of his here and now.

"Once in a while. I taught her to ride years ago. Her job keeps her pretty busy, though, so I generally exercise both horses whenever I'm home." Nicholas towed her farther inside the old building. "What I wanted to show you is over here."

The hay littering the floor grew deeper as they proceeded. They walked another few yards, and then Nicholas was telling her to kneel down and stretch out her hands.

Soft, mewing noises came to her ears, chorused by a
series of wiggly, scrambling sounds. Carefully she extended her fingers to brush across the frayed edges of
cardboard, then down inside a box. Several downy
balls of fur tumbled across her hands. One of the
squirmers met her seeking palms head-on and greeted
them with nuzzles and tentative, questing bites from
needle-sharp teeth.

"Kittens! Oh, Nicholas, they're so tiny! Are they old
enough to be held?"

"I hope so." He laughed. "I've been doing it all week."

The soothing murmurs trickling from Casi's throat
were as soft as the kittens' own mewing. She cupped
both hands, isolating one of the warm, wiggly shapes,
bringing it out of the cloth-lined box to cuddle against
her breast.

"Its eyes aren't open yet, but it seems willing to accept you as a friend," Nicholas observed as the kitten
vibrated contentedly in Casi's gentle grasp.

Poor little blind creature, she commiserated, feeling
a deep empathy with the tiny helpless animal. "The
mother won't abandon them, will she, or hide them
away?" she asked anxiously.

Nicholas assured her that wouldn't happen. "She's a
long-time pet who knows her brood will come to no
harm here. Love it all you want, Casi."

The change that had come over her face was incredible. Touched by her bemused expression, Nicholas
watched and felt his own eyes prickle with moisture.
She had been needing something like this, he thought.
Some risk-free way to indulge her loving nature. Casi
was too wary right now to lavish that affection on people. Him, in particular. But she had certainly opened
her heart to that kitten.

They stayed in the barn for almost an hour, holding and petting each of the kittens without any show of favoritism. Just about the time Nicholas began to have visions of Soledad's lunch congealing on the table, the mother cat stalked in and took charge, bumping against their legs in annoyance.

"Dinnertime for the young'uns," he said, setting the last kitten back inside the box where its mother could feed it. "And for us big people, too."

He placed both hands around Casi's waist to help her to her feet. She rose lightly, raising her arms automatically to use him for balance. Her upturned face hovered very near his. Unable to resist those beautiful lips, Nicholas enfolded her fragile body in the circle of his arms, bringing his mouth very tenderly down on hers.

Casi slid her arms up his brawny shoulders, marveling at the contrast between his hard sinews and the lightness of his embrace. The kiss was a gentle exchange, uncomplicated by passion, as feathery on her lips as the kitten had been in her hands. There was a reassurance to it, a wordless expression of contentment flowing from one to the other.

Almost immediately Nicholas drew away. "Soledad's expecting us," he murmured.

"It wouldn't be polite to keep her waiting," Casi agreed gravely. Could a whole hour have passed so swiftly? "I'm so glad you brought me out to the barn. The kittens are wonderful."

And so are you, each of them added in their hearts, though neither said anything more.

CASI STRETCHED OUT in bed that night, her mind on Nicholas. It was a temptation to believe that the man she had met before the bandages went over her eyes was just an imposter, masquerading under his name. That person had been magnetically attractive, but she hadn't really liked him. Yet the mere thought of today's companion gave her shivers of joy.

She reached toward the nightstand and picked up the two-way radio. For several minutes she ran her thumb along the little lever before pulling it back.

"Nicholas?" she said tentatively, wondering if the sound of her voice would really travel through the two sets of walls and down a hill.

There was an instant snap as the dead air came alive. "I'm here, Casi," he replied. "Do you need anything?"

"No. I just wanted to say thank-you for the lovely day."

"I enjoyed every minute of it. And guess what?"

"Hmm?"

"Tomorrow will be even better."

"How come?"

"You get to help me plant a vegetable garden, and then we're going fishing."

"Wow! I can't wait!"

She meant it, too. Now she understood why Melina was content to trot along behind him with the Band-Aids all those years ago. To spend some time with Nicholas, Casi was even willing to carry the worms!

6

CASI LIKED the way Nicholas smelled first thing in the morning. Of necessity, since it was his hand or arm she depended upon to guide her along, she spent a great deal of time in his immediate vicinity. Sharing air space with him was a pleasure. Whenever he came near she caught a mingled scent of piney soap, light after-shave and pungent leather. She always tried to take at least one long, deep breath of him before he spoke. After that her senses all too quickly became bewitched by the deep, richly masculine timbre of his voice.

His voice had its ups and downs. Like hers, it wasn't always confident. Sometimes she detected vulnerability there, an admission that he wasn't so sure about everything, either, in spite of what his words might proclaim. Occasionally there was a trace of sadness lingering in some cadence of his tone; impatience crept into an inflection now and then. More often, however, she caught laughter there. He'd even been known to poke fun at himself. It was easy to identify both affection and devotion whenever a member of his family was being discussed.

Little by little in the past ten days she had learned to differentiate the various nuances of his voice to tell her what sort of man Nicholas was deep down inside. Its pitch helped her gauge his moods, hinted at what sort of expression he wore, definitely indicated when she wasn't measuring up to his expectations.

Two months ago, if a new man had come into her life, she would have relied primarily on her vision to tell her all she thought she needed to know about him. External details would have been vitally important: hair and eye color, posture, his walk, the way he wore his clothes. Without a doubt she would have used the play of expressions across his face almost exclusively to decipher how he was reacting to her, placing far too much importance on smiles and frowns, raised eyebrows and beckoning glances.

That wasn't possible in this case. Not that there was anything wrong with her memory. When she stopped to think about it, less and less as the days went by, she could remember exactly how Nicholas looked. But stopping to picture his physical appearance nowadays was almost more of a hindrance than a help in getting to know him. The person her eyes had watched during their troubled working relationship had been reserved, disagreeable. The Nicholas she had met more recently—the man she could only hear and smell and touch—was definitely...nice. She thought about those two persons fairly often, and on reflection, she was convinced that her more recent impressions came closer to assessing the authentic Nicholas.

Casi made herself a promise. If she was lucky enough to have her sight restored, she would never go back to depending on sight alone. She would look, greedily fill her eyes . . . and then she would close them and begin to listen.

The question of how Nicholas really felt about her entered her mind often. He didn't hate her; she would have identified that emotion in his voice. But when it came to anything more positive, she was almost afraid to guess. His treatment of her was invariably gentle, sometimes extremely tender. But the fact that she had been warned about his guilt complex kept a nagging suspicion lingering in her thoughts. It was still possible that she was just another crusade for him.

He had never called her "sweetheart" again. Looking back, she believed now that the scene in her bedroom had been triggered by the terrific amount of stress they were both under at the time. That, and because of the way she had happened to be dressed. She was a darned attractive woman, Casi knew. She hadn't spent fourteen years adorning magazines for nothing. That morning he had wanted her as much as she had wanted him. But the satin nightgown had undoubtedly been the catalyst.

The day he had first taken her to visit his house he had let her know in no uncertain terms that someday... Casi's face grew hot as she remembered his words—his vow. It had never happened, though. Maybe he had thought better of the idea.

Most of the hours they spent together were focused on Nicholas's attempts to teach her self-reliance. She was constantly being encouraged to use her fingers, as well as her ears and nose and even her taste buds, to examine new situations and learn to cope with them. Deep in her heart, Casi knew that all this instruction had a very pointed purpose. He was terrified that she might wind up being permanently blind. As well as he could, he was trying to prepare her for future challenges.

Casi was terrified, too. Not only was she afraid of the outcome when the bandages came off this Friday, she was scared to death of losing Nicholas. She couldn't stay here forever, taking advantage of Melina's hospitality, but she couldn't conceive of how she would get by without him when it came time to leave. It wasn't just dependence linking her to him now. In their time together she had come to know Nicholas the sweet, thoughtful companion, Nicholas the patient instructor, Nicholas the worrier. And she had fallen deeply in love with all three of him.

The knowledge that hers was a one-sided love made her even more determined to channel her life into some useful new direction, which left her hauntingly afraid that this lofty goal would be forever beyond her reach. During many of each day's quiet moments, Casi was tormented by the awareness that even should she regain her eyesight, she could never return to the familiar security of her former profession. Worse still, the motion of existing in dark do-nothingness for long, useless years intruded into her nighttime hours, coloring ordinary dreams a nightmarish black.

But self-pity was an emotion she refused to succumb to. Firmly Casi forced her mental energies into trying to formulate a contingency plan for the future. Some stimulating new focus on life had become a drastic necessity. Unfortunately her new occupation would have to do more than merely take the place of modeling. It would have to be fascinating enough, engrossing enough to compensate for the void in her private life, as well.

With a twinge of bitterness, Casi wondered just how far career retraining had come nowadays. Not far enough, she suspected gloomily. No matter how challenging, any new job she might learn to master would only be runner-up to what she really wanted to do. That, of course, was to love Nicholas with all her heart and soul, to know that he reciprocated that feeling and to stand next to him, on her own two feet, as together they coped with life's problems.

Her few brief infatuations of the past couldn't begin to measure up to the power of her feelings where he was concerned. She was very much afraid that the old Cavanaugh curse had struck her at last. But if she was going to be a one-man woman, she just wished she hadn't picked someone who only felt sorry for her.

Trying to be honest, she admitted that that was the real core of their relationship. He was sorry for her, and he meant to teach her to cope with life in the dark, whether she wanted to learn or not.

Like last night.

She had been tired, edgy. There had been people around all weekend, old friends of the family, including Olivia, whom she had encountered for the first time that Sunday afternoon. The park ranger had a pleasantly melodious voice; a light, quick step; cool, gentle fingers when shaking hands. Everything about her was young. She sounded beautiful, especially when she spoke to Nicholas. Having grown accustomed to listening with all her might, Casi had no difficulty at all in hearing the affection that crept in when the girl's words were addressed to him.

By evening the effort of trying to appear serene and normal all day had sharpened into fatigue. Nicholas, whose timing was usually better, had waited until the company left and then decided it was time she learned to use a telephone.

At first Casi gave it her all. There was nothing hard about manipulating a push-button phone. With the buttons lined up in threes, a bright two-year-old could have done it, she told herself. It was the strain of trying to remember the number she was supposed to be dialing *plus* keeping count of how many digits she had already punched *plus* trying to figure out where her fingers should land to hit an eight or four that had gotten to her at last.

"I don't want to do this right now," she told him in exasperation. "I'm tired of trying to keep everything straight in my head."

"Do it for me just once. Then I'll go home," he coaxed.

Casi's fingers felt nervous and jerky. That probably had a lot to do with her sharp tone of voice. "I said I didn't want to fool with this thing anymore!"

"Look, I know how you feel—"

The short fuse she was on hit the detonator. "No, you don't!" she heard herself shouting. "You don't really know how I feel, Nicholas, because all you have to do is open your eyes when you want to see something. The phone number, for example, would be right there in front of you if you forgot whether the last group was 7329 or 7923. When you can't remember where you left your shoes, you just stand up and look around. I get down on the floor and crawl, thumping the corners. If you want to—"

"I get the message," he interrupted quickly. "You sound pretty tired. I'll see you tomorrow."

She had an impulse to growl that he might see her, but she wouldn't be able to return the favor. With a gigantic effort Casi restrained herself. She slammed out of the room, heading for bed even before he left the Jorgensens' house. For the first time since he had presented it to her, she didn't pick up the radio to tell him good-night.

Now, the next morning, she wondered whether he was coming; he had always arrived before she even got out of bed. It just felt late, Casi told herself. She'd had three cups of coffee, swallowed down some orange juice and listened to the morning news roundup. She could easily have turned on the radio again to find out what time it was, but she didn't want to do that. She wanted things to continue as they had been.

Hurt, stubborn pride prevented her from turning the lever on the communicator. The trouble was, she'd grown too dependent on him. That couldn't go on for more than a few days longer at best. She knew it was time she started weaning herself away from his constant guidance. Common sense told her that Nicholas must have better things to do than continue to be her keeper. But surely he would have said something, prepared her.

Jittery fingers picked up the little plastic radio again and fiddled with the lever. Her heart bellowed for her to turn it and call out to him. Self-respect said, "Don't you dare!" She compromised by taking it along when she went outside to sit on the front porch.

By now Casi had become highly adept at finding her way around Melina's house. Unfalteringly she walked across the tile entryway, turned the doorknob and continued out to perch on the top step.

It was another gorgeous day. March in California bore no resemblance to that ghastly month in New York. The sun was still behind the house, but the air didn't have that damp, foggy thickness to it she had tasted a few times. The trees were full of birds squabbling over who was going to get which branch for which nest. There was just enough breeze whispering along the road to clearly convey the sound of the ocean without kicking up the dust. It mingled the scents of wildflowers and lumber, wafting them toward her on light, caressing waves.

The wind stirred again and presented her with a new sound. Footsteps. Slow, wavering, unsteady.

Casi raised her head to listen intently. The footsteps were heavy—a man's. She knew Vasco's walk by now, as well as the confident strides that always told her when Nicholas or Dane was approaching. This was a private section of road. Ordinarily strangers didn't trespass. Yet nobody called out a greeting, as they would have done if someone she knew had caught sight of her sitting there. In truth, the unsteady gait sounded like the steps of a person weaving around in an alcoholic stupor. A wino? Some vagrant who stopped now and then to tilt a bottle to his lips?

The sound grew more pronounced, then changed texture as soles raked across gravel rather than dirt.

"Who's there?" she called nervously.

"It's just me, Casi," she heard Nicholas reply. "What are you doing outside?"

Relief hit her. She set down the radio and strained toward his oncoming sound.

"Waiting for you." Listening to those uncertain steps, she grew apprehensive all over again. "That doesn't really sound like you, Nicholas. Your footsteps are all staggery. Are you—"

"Keep talking. I'm coming."

Drunk or injured, one or the other, she thought in sudden panic. But even at night he seldom had more than a glass or two of wine.

"What do you mean, 'keep talking'? I'm sitting right here where you can see me!" Her voice quavered with anxiety. "Nicholas, what happened? Did you hurt yourself?"

There was no answer, though he was close enough now for his ragged breathing to rasp on her ears. She heard the sound of leather striking wood, followed by a heavy thud.

Casi let out a terrified scream. "Oh, my God, you *are* hurt!" She grabbed for him, sending a flurry of pats toward his head and chest.

"It's okay. Quit worrying. I'm just fine," Nicholas panted.

"You aren't, either. You never sounded like this before!" Casi was half-hysterical by now. "I can't feel any blood. Nicholas, where—"

He grabbed her hands to stop their frantic flutters. "There isn't any blood. I am perfectly all right." He emphasized the words one by one to calm her down. "If you'll quit swatting at me, I'll tell you what this is all about, okay?"

Her chin was wobbling, but the fright had started to recede. Nicholas wouldn't lie to her. His voice sounded normal enough now, and he'd sworn he wasn't injured.

"You scared me half to death," she said, hearing a tremor in the accusation.

"I'm sorry. Honest, I didn't know you were out here. I wouldn't have—" He brought her hands up to his lips. "Casi, I was trying an experiment, that's all. Last night I stupidly said I knew how you felt, and you lost your temper and hollered that I didn't, that I couldn't. So I . . . thought I'd find out." Nicholas groaned. "Boy, did I find out!"

One hand escaped him to zero in on his face. Her searching fingers encountered a folded cloth stretched tightly over his eyes. She let out a gasp.

"Nicholas Penheiro, did you walk all the way over here without being able to see where you were going? What if you'd fallen down the cliff?"

"I'd have had it coming." He sounded embarrassed. "The idea came to me on the way home last night. I went breezing along, making big-shot plans so I could come back today and brag that all a person had to do was set his mind on something. . . ."

"Did you trip over things?"

"Every time I got out of the chair. I have the most painful bruises...." It sounded as if Nicholas preferred not to go into all the gory details. "For my final trick of the evening I sat down and tried dialing my phone number. My own number! I reached three irate home-owners, the Orpheum Theater and some place called 'Manny's.' It sounded like a bar in the roughest part of Oakland." His head waggled in disgust. "Honey, compared to you, I'm a klutz. I felt 'useless, useless, useless'!"

How well Casi remembered that phrase. Gently she tugged at the folded handkerchief, visualizing it as one of those oversized types farmers use, red or dark blue.

"Nicholas, you're forgetting something."

"I don't doubt it a bit. Any man who could forget his own phone number—"

"You didn't have a patient teacher to shove you in the right direction. I've had you to guide me around, to show me how to use my hands and ears and nose. Without you I'd be in there yet, pounding the carpet."

His arms went around her shoulders. "Casi, darling..."

"Honey" and "darling" both in the space of five minutes; the experience must have unhinged him, she thought. Then his lips descended across hers, and the force of their ardent pressure made rational cogitation out of the question. There was nothing gentle about this particular show of affection.

Casi kissed him back. She let her lips roam across his, allowed her mouth to close on the fullness of his with a passion that both astonished and enraptured her. Then she made room for the thrusting quest of his tongue and responded with a flickering dart of her own against it.

"Umm, Nicholas," she moaned when his lips finally released her mouth and began distributing quick kisses along her curving cheeks, her uptilted nose, around her ear.

"Umm, Casi!"

Both hands cradled her chin, drawing her face so close to his that she could feel his breath warming her. When their mouths came together a second time, she raised her hands to the back of his head, running her fingers through his thick, wavy hair. She curled them around his neck, gorged herself on the feel of his skin, touched him as she had longed to touch him for days and days and days. . . .

Nicholas moved back a tiny fraction. "Casi?" he murmured against her mouth.

"I think this is me," she responded groggily, straining for the return of his lips.

"Remember what you said to me once about the time and the place?" He swung her up into his arms. "I've just thought of the perfect solution to that problem."

Casi in his arms, Nicholas began to jog down the gravel path. "Where are we going?" she murmured, rubbing her cheek against his.

"My house. It's a good place. Any objections?"

"Not . . . one."

"Good." From the sound of his voice, neither arguments nor kicking and screaming would have been to much avail had Casi disagreed.

There was little chance of that, however. She wouldn't have allowed a crowbar to pry her loose from his grip. "Now that you've solved the place, what about the time," she wondered out loud.

"It's about 10:45. Will that do?"

"It'll probably have to. Unless you've got at least two full vases of cold water sitting around on an end table somewhere."

He halted in the middle of the road to kiss her again. "You remember Noah's flood?"

"Vaguely." It was hard to remember anything with his lips so close to hers.

"Even that much cold water wouldn't have any effect this time."

Shadows absorbed the sunlight from her face as he marched up the steps of his house. Her previous visits had been confined to kitchen and patio. Now, when the huge oak door was thrown open and his footsteps sounded on the parquet of the entry hall, they turned in the opposite direction. A dozen long strides bore them down a corridor. He opened a door, marched through it with her still in his arms and hooked it shut with his elbow. Advancing a few paces, he set her down on a bed.

The covers were already turned back. Rather self-consciously she ran her hand over the sheet.

Pulling off his boots, Nicholas sat down beside her. "Believe it or not, I'm usually a good housekeeper. As a rule, I don't go off leaving the bed unmade. But as soon as I got up this morning, I started mowing down furniture again. I didn't have the courage to tackle another chore in my condition. All I wanted was to get to you, tell you . . . tell you everything."

Tenderly Casi reached up and took his face between her hands. She touched his eyelids, then smoothed her fingers toward his temples where indentations still marked the placement of the bandanna. The welts were deeply creased, as though the cloth had had a long time to pinch into his flesh.

"Did you sleep with that awful thing around your head all night?" she asked, incredulous that he would have gone to such lengths.

Nicholas's hands touched the side of her own face where the bandage was strapped. "Don't you? I told you, Casi. I was literally trying to find out how you felt, to learn exactly how it would affect a person to be cut off from light, to be prevented from knowing what was happening three feet out in front."

"So now you know."

"No, sweetheart, not really." Underneath her hands she could feel the negative shake of his head. "I wore it for about fourteen hours, from 8:30 last night until I stumbled up to you this morning. I won't say that was the worst stretch of my life. That took place the night I sat in the hospital, waiting for them to bring you out of the operating room. But it was pretty bad. I tried to do half a dozen of the things I'd watched you master, and couldn't cope with any one of them. It was one of the most frustrating, humiliating experiences I've ever had to endure. But I still couldn't put myself in your place, because all the time I knew that I only had to reach up and untie the bandanna and I'd have my sight back again."

Casi tried to swallow around the obstacle in her throat. "You're quite a teacher, you know that? There aren't many who would go out and get that kind of field experience."

"I'm no teacher," Nicholas said quietly. "I'm just the man who's in love with you."

She snatched her hands back as though they'd been burned, dropping them into her lap. The mattress beneath them jiggled with shock waves from the abruptness of her action. Unable to speak, she sat there, even white teeth clenching her lip.

"You don't believe me, do you?" he asked after a moment. "Don't ever go into the intrigue business, Casi. Stay out of high-stakes poker games, too. That face would give you away every time."

"Oh, I—" She shook her head, clearing it, and tried to rearrange her expression. "You took me by surprise. That was absolutely the last thing in the world I was expecting."

Nicholas leaned over and took the hands out of her lap. "Honey, you don't lie worth a damn. Want me to tell you what you were thinking just then? It went something like this. 'That can't possibly be true. He's only saying that because he feels sorry for me, because it's his fault I can't see and now he's had a taste of how terrible that condition truly is.'" He paused. "How close did I come, Casi?"

She drew a deep breath, feeling the rush of color to her cheeks. The guess had hit home. On the night of her arrival Dane had made a similar shrewd assessment of her innermost thoughts, and she'd been moved to ask him where he kept his crystal ball. She must have a face that practically drew viewers a map from A to B.

"You were off by a syllable or two," she admitted in acute embarrassment.

"Thank you," Nicholas said. "I do like a truthful woman."

"Could— Is there any chance we could start again? Come through the door and pretend we just got here?"

"We made a pact on the beach. This relationship was to be kept moving forward, not back. Remember?"

She nodded miserably. "So where does that leave us?"

"With the time and the place. We have reached that stage, haven't we?"

"I—" Casi thought better of trying to lie. "Yes."

"It also leaves us with a man who has just told a woman that he loves her. And with a woman who doesn't believe him. Not because she doesn't want to." Nicholas watched as Casi's face flared absolutely scarlet. "Only because she has some understandable doubts about his truthfulness. So...I think what he should do is try to convince her."

Casi's emotions were zooming up and down. His tone was the most sincere sound she had heard in her whole life.

"I've never known anyone like you," she gasped. "I practically insult you in my thoughts, and—"

"Let's talk about it later," Nicholas interrupted. "We've been talking for ten days. But as you just reminded me, it's easy for some people to say one thing and mean something else entirely. Since that approach is under suspicion, I propose we try a different way of getting through to each other. Popularly known as the 'hands on' method."

"I put my hands on you, you put your hands on me, and neither of us does any mind reading, right?"

"Right," Nicholas fibbed. "Ladies first."

7

TENTATIVELY Casi raised one hand to his face. Questing fingertips inched across his brow, marking the furrows there. The bristly strands of thick, slashing eyebrows flowed beneath her touch. Almost absently she brought her other hand up to join its companion in a bemused exploration of his countenance. Yes, she thought, this was the face she remembered seeing. But it wasn't so stern now. It seemed more . . . tranquil.

In delicate strokes she smoothed her way across his closed eyelids, mourning the hours his sight had lost, the painful confusion he had suffered, thanking him for the noble, most generous effort he had made to fully understand the extent of her handicap. The curl of his lashes feathered past. A shiver ran down her back.

"It's not cold in here," Nicholas pointed out.

"Hush! I'm concentrating." Casi's fingers found the laugh lines that crinkled at the sides of his eyes. Above them were small indentations, hollows just large enough for a pair of lips to snuggle into. She caressed the twin areas with a gentle rain of kisses from her soul and was tempted to let her fingertips linger there indefinitely. But the rest of his face beckoned her to continue. Her hands moved along clean-shaven cheeks, down the sweep of his nose, high bridged and straight. His nostrils flared slightly. She remembered how arrogant that nose had seemed at times. Beneath it was a tiny dip in line with the center of his mouth.

Without realizing what she was doing, Casi let her tongue flicker briefly across the moist edge of her own lower lip.

Watching that tongue curve unconsciously around her lip, Nicholas steeled himself to remain still and allow her to concentrate. It was a terrible effort to keep his mouth away from hers about ninety percent of the time, anyway, but when she did things like that . . .

He'd known before that he had the power to arouse her. Ten days ago, when he had lost control of himself and gathered her into his arms in Melina's guest room, there had been a number of outward signs pointing in that direction. But that day they had come together on the rebound from other powerful emotions, and although at the time he suspected her hunger was as great as his, she had stopped him. Since then he had been working desperately to gain her trust, build her affection toward him. Nicholas wasn't willing to settle for desire alone. That was much too fleeting. He wanted her permanently. For that to work, there had to be a great deal more than momentary desire on her part. Something much, much deeper.

Her intensity was beautiful to behold. She was really putting her heart into becoming intimately reacquainted with his features. With her eyes covered, however, it was very difficult to determine whether there was anything besides just plain wanting tucked away in her feelings toward him.

Fortunately, unlike Casi, Nicholas didn't have to rely exclusively on tonal nuances to try to guess what she was thinking. He regarded her upturned face almost analytically, seeking some flicker of expression to tell him what he really wanted to know.

Casi had already been introduced to the full, mobile softness of Nicholas's lips. While she yearned to discover them all over again in this different method of knowing, to measure their exact outline, to seal finger kisses across them, she restrained herself for the moment. "Deferred gratification," she believed psychologists called that ploy. Making the experience sweeter when the time finally did arrive.

Her fingers moved right and left over the planes of his face to swoop along the slanting arc of his sideburns. The symmetry of them pleased her. So did the aesthetic contrast of their shape. She retraced them again and again with the rounded edges of her nails, enjoying the texture of the hair. It was oddly sensual—arousing. Everything about this man seemed to turn her on. . . .

Casi's jaw muscles tightened, tamping down a piercingly primitive burst of desire that had begun to tremble deep within her. *Enough of that*, she warned herself. Too quickly for Nicholas to intercept that tantalizing thought, she swept her hands away, moving over to the ridgy spirals of his ears. Daintily she investigated the crevices folded within, smoothed across the flesh of his lobes. Her hands flowed downward, then back up to massage the sensitive area just below his ears.

With grim determination Nicholas centered his mind on cold water, icy liquid. He tried to regulate his breathing so she wouldn't suspect what this was doing to him. They had only just begun and already a geyser of steam was building deep in his loins.

Her hands trailed down either side of his jawbone, studiously avoiding the sideburns, to meet at the point of his chin. That chin could jut with the best of them when it was in the mood, Casi knew. It had a habit of thrusting obstinately forward in challenge. But now the muscles forcing the belligerent tilt were relaxed.

She had saved the best for last. A filmy sheen of perspiration broke out, dappling the top of her upper lip as she fluted one forefinger around his mouth, taking time to examine all the lines, the dips, the curves. These were lips that could smile. How could she ever have found them harsh and implacable?

The inner edge of his upper lip felt invitingly moist. Unconsciously angling her head an inch or two to the left, Casi trailed a lone finger across the inside of it, grazing it off the straight, polished shapes of his teeth, while her middle finger echoed the movement across the lower portion of his mouth.

Nicholas's tongue decided to investigate the intrusion. In the kind of lick he might have given a strawberry ice-cream cone, it swept the length of the finger. Then, with an insidious sucking motion, he drew the forefinger inside to be stimulatingly massaged.

Casi didn't think she could take much more. In another minute she was going to start tearing off his clothes, and there would go the experiment. With an intake of breath that was almost a gasp, she dropped her hand.

Nicholas chuckled wickedly. "And that's only the beginning. There's a great deal more of me."

"A slow process like that is liable to take all day," she sighed, resisting the impulse to squirm.

"It's our time, Casi. Let's squander a little more of it."

The mattress shifted slightly as he brought his hands up to take their turn. "Now that we've both gotten a tiny inkling of how I feel to your fingers, I'm hoping this will give you a clue about my emotions where you're concerned."

"How could—"

"Sh," he murmured. "Pay attention."

Nicholas used both hands from the very beginning. They were large, powerful hands, capable of dealing firmly with almost any situation. A person who looked at them, Casi remembered, tended to picture karate chops, judo holds, right hooks. But now they displayed an amazingly deft versatility when stealing up around the sides of her neck to the divided hollow at her nape.

A single finger drew slow, vertical strokes from base to hairline, sweeping up, petting. Thumbs joined two fingers in a dexterous survey of a few wispy auburn tendrils clustered there. Grasping them, fluting them, drawing them down with barely enough tension to cause her skin to prickle in sensuous response, he smoothed out the short strands and fluttered them in a whisperingly soft tease across the back of her neck. Then the fingers swept unhurriedly along her hairline to curl up beneath her ears. They paused there, massaging the delicate hollows underneath with consummate skill.

Casi could no more keep from reacting to this stimulation than the sun could help rising in the east. Earthquake country around here, she recalled as a tremor rocked her. But the house didn't lurch; nor did the floor buckle. Something told her no mere cataclysm was responsible for the upheaval.

Lord, how she loved what he was doing to her, how she loved him. And she would gladly have given up another sense to be able to believe that he truly loved her. If only this moment could last an eternity. Because she needed him forever, ached for him to want her always.

At last Nicholas saw what he'd been watching for. *Now I know. Now I'm sure,* he thought. He was able to close his eyes in relief as he continued to caress her.

Somehow, in spite of the beast he had been, the horrible accident he had caused, she had fallen in love with him. The knowledge was the most precious gift he had ever received.

How many years had he been aching to have her? It was impossible to remember. All his life, it seemed. And now he realized he needed a lifetime with her, fifty-seven years at least, as his grandfather and Luisita had had.

He wanted her, and he wanted her children. He could almost picture them, little redheaded Penheiros with the Cavanaugh look. He wanted them desperately. But if, like Jeanne, she wasn't willing to burden that sleek shapely body of hers with bearing them, he'd settle for being an uncle. He had never wanted anybody, anything, as much as he wanted Casi.

Nicholas swiveled the tip of his forefinger in agonizingly slow movements along her upper lip. With repeated, loving strokes he burnished the tender skin there, kissing her by proxy. To his delight her lips puckered delicately, blowing kisses back at him as if feeling his imaginary ones. His finger followed the bowed curve, up and around and down.

Casi parted her teeth and nibbled. She was only beginning to savor the taste of him, though, when the finger escaped and dampness trailed downward. He drew it across her bottom lip, bisected her chin and let it maraud underneath. It flowed as though pulled by gravity, to drop into the hollow of her throat. There it began an insidious spiral.

"You're practicing witchcraft," she breathed.

"Uh-huh," Nicholas affirmed. "I need an edge to help me make my point."

"You've already made your point," Casi murmured. "This is the time."

"That's *our* point. My personal point is that I love you. Words couldn't convince you of the depth of my feelings toward you. Has what I've been telling you with my hands helped you to accept the truth?"

Casi couldn't seem to catch her breath. She had been paying attention to every nuance of his touch in the same way that her ears strained for inflections in his voice. What she had felt there had shaken her faith in logic. "Your hands make me want to believe," she whispered.

It was a start, Nicholas told himself. He had won the preliminary bout with her doubts, but it was going to be an uphill fight to the championship. He removed his finger from her throat and directed his hand downward to seek her breast. His lips began to caress her mouth in the same convincingly passionate way that his finger had done a moment before.

He kissed sensationally well, Casi thought. Literally. Every movement of Nicholas's mouth across hers created sensory havoc within her, causing a domino effect. Restless prickles started gathering as far down as her ankles, sending out alarms, alerting muscles and nerve endings en route to the center of her body.

Through the fleecy thickness of her sweatshirt she could feel the heat generating from his palm, seeping through the cloth and being massaged deeply into her skin. Her swollen nipple was making a point of its own as the hand spiraled around the contours surrounding it. The hardening nub seemed to be trying to flag down his slightly curved fingers, begging them for some attention. On every pass, though, he just seemed to miss it.

Casi squirmed in torment, wanting more, wanting everything.

With her mouth locked against his, she began using her tongue to make Nicholas aware of the riot he was inciting within her. *Make love to me, Nicholas,* Casi pleaded silently. *Right now,* her fingers implored. *Take me, Nicholas, my darling, my love. I want you so much.*

Some of her impatience seemed to transmit itself to him. Either that, or a growing urgency of his own impelled him to slide his hand away from her breast and tug upward on the hem of her shirt.

Casi unwrapped her arms from him. She used her hands to help him, making sure the bandage stayed in place, all the while thinking how much she wanted to feast on him with her eyes, experience him with every sense, not just the four she had left. But beggars couldn't be choosers. She intended to use everything she still had at her command to make the most of the occasion.

She ducked inside the sweatshirt, bowing for a moment while Nicholas rolled it up over her eyes and back across her head. He didn't seem to be in any hurry yet to free her arms from the sleeves, however. He continued to draw the shirt in reverse with just enough pressure to make her arms twine around behind her. Her torso arched toward him as her arms continued to be extended behind her back until her two palms were almost touching and her head tipped backward, hair spilling in a flaming curtain across the bare white rounded forearms. With the tilting of her body her breasts belled out, straining toward him as her back arched in a graceful curve. The momentary pose gave her the appearance of a figurehead on a sailing ship of old.

Hungrily Nicholas took in the mounded curves, not so lavish as they had been before her stay in the hospital, but no longer cotton candy, either. He felt his blood start to bubble at the sight of those straining points.

Some ancient sea dog from the past whispered that while his figurehead's bosom might have been lovingly carved wood rather than throbbing human flesh, at least it had not been restrained by fripperies such as lace. Nicholas got the message. He quickly pulled the sweatshirt the rest of the way past her hands, dropped it and bent to unclip the front closing of her bra. Lifting the garment away, he realized that the lusty old corsair had been right. Her breasts were firm, beautifully rounded, studded in the centers by nipples the delectible shade of raspberries. They were so seductively thrusting that it was all he could do to keep his mouth off them.

He battered down the surging impulse. This was going to be done slowly, and it was going to be done right. There mightn't be another opportunity before Friday to convince her of his love. After that, it might very well be too late. During their rocky acquaintance he'd been given a few samples of that stubborn Irish pride of hers. If the laser surgery wasn't successful she would never agree to be his wife. He had to get her to accept him first . . . before the bandages were removed. Their entire futures were riding on his powers of persuasion.

The moment her arms were released Casi dived for his buttons. Knowing nothing about his figurehead fantasy or the concerns keeping Nicholas's seduction of her from proceeding as quickly as either of them really desired, she had nevertheless interpreted his silence to mean that his eyes were fully occupied. Her fingers fumbled with the slippery rounds, the tightly corded holes. Cursing the sadistic makers of men's clothing, she felt an almost overpowering urge to bite the buttons loose from their threads.

He could look—she needed at least to touch!

"Your tongue's crept out again," Nicholas mentioned, bending to sugarcoat it with his own.

"Pay no attention to it. That always happens whenever I'm concentrating on a difficult task."

Casi found the continuing glide of his tongue across hers highly distracting. So far she had managed to make her way around only two of the buttons. It was frustrating, wanting to bare his chest and to keep on licking back at him at the same time.

"I can't concentrate, darling, not with you doing that," she groaned, keeping her tongue firmly inside to give her fingers priority.

In four seconds flat Nicholas had the rest of the buttons undone and had torn off his shirt.

"That's the first tender name I've coaxed out of you, do you realize that?" he asked, speaking over the triphammering thud of his heart. He slid off the mattress and scooped his hands underneath her bottom. "Stand up beside me."

Gladly Casi obliged, darting her hands forward as she rose. Her fingers buried themselves in the curly hair of his chest. An electric crackle added sound effects to the motion. She could almost picture jagged blue streaks shooting out from beneath her fingertips.

"Static electricity," Nicholas said with a laugh. "If contact as minor as that can draw sparks, can you imagine what's going to happen in a little while?"

"I hope this place is well grounded," Casi murmured, trying to keep her enticing fantasies at bay for a little while longer.

His hands came around to the front of her wrist. The snap of her jeans popped open; the zipper whirred down. Tracing her middle, his hands glided behind her. On each side four fingers wiggled down inside the waistbands of denim and lace; all eight fingers descended in roving unison along her hips. They traveled in slow motion out around the swelling flare of her buttocks, molding the shape of them for an instant or two, before moving down her thighs.

Risking more sparks, Casi ran her hands down the tapering line of crisp hair to his belt. The texture of the furry mat across his chest entranced her; she wasn't anywhere near finished appreciating it yet. But there were other things to be done. Finding the end of his belt, she reversed the oval leather tab through the buckle and tugged, crooking her right forefinger to release the hook. Ten days of lessons in manual dexterity had finally paid off, she thought in satisfaction.

Now that it was undone she ignored the leather belt, letting it hang loosely in its loops. Instead she zeroed in on the center of him again to deal with a snap and a zipper even more efficiently than he had handled hers. And her job was far trickier, she decided. The tab she drew downward had to be maneuvered around the pressure of bulging masculinity.

Casi hooked her thumbs inside the waistband of his jeans, following it around to the middle of his lower back. She bumped them along his lowest vertabra and tattooed an interesting evasion pattern across him with the edge of those two nails while she pulled down.

Nicholas drew her toward him as they shimmied the rest of the way out of their clothing and kicked it aside. Holding her by the shoulders, he measured her height against his own.

"Yes, I know I'm tall," Casi drawled, reading his mind for a change.

"Spectacularly so. I can't imagine why I ever thought short girls were any fun. Feel what happens when our bodies come together?"

Casi bumped into him in several places simultaneously, but it was a gentle, sensuous collision. "We touch?"

"In all the right spots. Perfect fit."

Her temperature shot up another notch as Nicholas demonstrated his meaning. Her shoulders were moved seductively back and forth, carrying the rest of her body along with them. Little corkscrews of chest hair brushed against straining nipples, tickling them into an even higher erection. Flat bellies massaged each other. The hardness of him inscribed a warm, deliberate line from the point of one hipbone to the other.

Nicholas's hands left her shoulders and began a body search. In a leisurely manner they sauntered across her contours, examining every curve and hollow. The light, trailing motion glided without pausing to seek.

It occurred to Casi then that she hadn't finished "looking" at Nicholas using the hands-on technique they'd been practicing. Starting with the sweep of his shoulders, she began an inching, muscle-by-muscle perusal. With light pinches she tormented his small hard nipples, wondering what kind of miracle alloy his willpower was made of. If he really was a mind reader, she speculated, maybe she could telegraph the idea that she was ready for that "let's talk about it later" stage of this encounter. She let her fingers explore the curve of one rib with slow-motion thoroughness.

When Nicholas spoke, his voice sounded a bit strangulated. "You said yourself that a process like that was liable to take all day."

"Hours, at least. You'd rather it didn't?" Casi asked guilelessly.

"All day would be fine." Nicholas almost groaned the words. "All day tomorrow, all day Wednesday..."

With that she was lifted in his arms and carried forward, then laid gently across the sheet. In another instant the length of his body was beside her.

Casi's hand smoothed over the indentation of his navel. "Nicholas..."

"Shh. Let me love you," he said, beginning to caress her with his lips.

With consummate artistry his mouth retraced the route his hands had recently taken. There was a subtle difference in these movements, however. Where the hands had merely glided, the lips took the opportunity to press fervent kisses at each pause along the way. Where the fingertips had slid, the tongue burned a trail. Where his nails had brushed, his teeth took tiny, painless bites that left radiating tingles in their wake.

He savored the taste of her warm, throbbing, gardenia-scented flesh, using his iron will to keep the rampaging fires of his own body under stern control. He had made love to many women in the past, Nicholas thought, but never like this. Never with the deliberate arousal tactics he was using on this glowing, now wonderfully pliant woman. If it caused him to explode, he was going to bring forth her pleasure first. He intended to make this experience of knowing him fully a total rapture for her without even considering—yet—what rapture having her would be for him.

Casi was quickly becoming aroused almost to the point of screaming, but Nicholas's wickedly magical hands kept finding new ways to make her writhe in ecstasy. He had to be suffering from his own urgent need for release, she thought dizzily. Yet he was deliberately staving it off, prolonging each and every sensation, causing exquisitely painful pleasure to engulf her. He must love her to do this....

His tongue painted a moist line down her cleavage. Casi gasped and arched toward him, her hands clenched into fists as his mouth moved along the lower curve of her breast. He nudged up the soft flesh, heating it with an erotic tingle of his tongue, and then his lips took over, laying down kisses that felt like the scorching imprints from a branding iron.

They needed a copyright, those kisses, Casi thought frantically. *Nobody* kissed like that except Nicholas!

His mouth sought the center of her breast and traced the quivering nipple. She felt it being sucked in between his lips the way he had tugged her finger into his mouth earlier, felt his tongue whirl and vibrate. Fire shot through her, rocketing out in all directions from that feverish point of contact.

Moaning with the torment of unfulfilled desire, she rocked her hips back and forth. Her thighs opened in an unconscious invitation and she reached out with both hands, wanting him, needing him desperately. Her fingers closed around the long spear of him. She felt pulsating movement as she layered her palms across the hard flesh, curling her fingers around to stroke, urging him to come to her.

"Not yet," Nicholas begged. "Don't do that yet or I won't have the strength to finish what I started."

"Nicholas, I'm going crazy!"

"Hold off," he whispered. "Wait for it, Casi. There's more. Relax now. Enjoy."

His mouth bent low to seek the other nipple, while his hand trailed down her abdomen, ruffling against flame-colored hair. It probed through the silken strands, seeking the core of her femininity. The sensually intimate massage caused Saturn's rings to whirl around in her head as his slowly undulating fingers caressed her into a frenzied pool of need.

Casi flung her hands back against the sheet. Her shoulders strained to bury themselves in the mattress, while reflexive muscles arched her torso upward. She tilted her chin, swinging her head from side to side as the wellspring of her moisture merged with his fingers to oil the friction, fuel the blaze.

She could feel her body rising while his other hand stroked erotically up the inner softness of her thigh. Her tongue flickered across her lips. Prickling, gloriously abundant sensations were ringing out in ever-widening circles from the very center of her being.

A gloss of perspiration dewdropped her skin. The tiny beads seemed to sizzle across her on the outside as every nerve in her body was sizzling inside. She had never come this far before, Casi thought wildly, never known there was such a fantastically powerful sensation in existence!

And still the tension within her kept building, heightening with excruciating intensity. She was so close, so close....

She caught her breath, low sensuous moans pouring from her constricted throat. Over her own sounds she could hear Nicholas's encouragement, urging her to soar, take wing and fly. Suddenly a dazzling atomic blast ruptured inside her. It created light she could actually see and feel and touch and taste; it was a roaring explosion she could hear.

"Nicholas, please!" she implored, almost insane with desire for the fulfillment of their union. With shaking hands she reached for him again, welcoming, guiding him home as her own pulsating throbs continued and spiraled anew at the touch of him against her threshold.

Invited by her trembling hands, Nicholas at last began his own quest for release. He found her with light jabs at first, then thrust deeper, filling her completely. Fierce, heaving thrusts rocked her slim form, propelling her even higher and higher toward the top of the bed. His toiling body mingled with hers in a passionate communion of love and desire, until at last they reached a fevered climax together.

8

FOR FULLY TEN MINUTES AFTERWARD Casi simply held him. She twined her arms around his shoulders and nestled his head against her cheek, loving him. Today she distinctly heard the clink of shining armor. Darned if Lancelot hadn't finally arrived.

She slicked her hands across his perspiring back. "Nicholas?" she whispered, not certain whether he was asleep or merely drugged with exhaustion. "Can you kick the sheet up to where I can reach it? We're both absolutely drenched. If we don't cover up, the next shiver we feel may be from pneumonia."

There was a thrashing flurry of kicks from the bottom of the bed. The poor mattress would never be the same again, she thought, stretching her fingers down to grab the sheet and drape it over him. She used the cool percale to blot some of the dampness from his skin.

The movements seemed to revive Nicholas. He levered himself backward, propping himself up on his elbows to remove some of his weight from her delicate torso.

"Well?" he asked.

"Darling, I'm too tired to clap," Casi murmured. "The best I can do is shout olé!"

"You know that's not what I meant! Casi, do you believe me now? Have you gotten it through that beautiful red head that I love you?"

"I rather think you must be telling the truth," she said, nodding. "Either that or you're the most generous man alive. I don't know how you held off— Nicholas, that was a simply incredible experience. I've never been made love to like that before."

"You inspire me to greatness. And the feeling was mutual." He brought his face down to hers, pressing his long, straight nose against her uptilted one. "What's this 'I rather think' stuff? You still aren't sure?"

"Yes, I'm sure. Positive."

"Say it, then. Out loud."

"I believe that Nicholas Penheiro means it when he says he loves Casi Cavanaugh. I am one hundred percent free of doubts. Lead me to a notary and I'll let him put his bumpy little seal over my signature to that effect."

"It's about time," he growled. "And how does Casi Cavanaugh feel about Nicholas Penheiro?"

"You're the mind reader." She laughed softly. "Don't you know?"

"Men as well as women need constant reinforcement to bolster their morale." He bumped her nose again. "*How...does...Casi...feel...about...Nicholas?*"

"She's crazy about him. Out of her mind over the man." Her fingers moved across his back, caressing every muscle they encountered. "I love you, Nicholas. Deep down, without ever realizing it, I think I've been in love with you for years. That's why nobody else I met ever made it to first place with me. I was comparing them to you, and they simply didn't measure up."

His lips traced the line of her jaw, around to her ear. "Don't exaggerate. You only met me last month."

"In person, yes. But back in that apartment we shared Melina always kept a big portrait of you on her dresser.

Not a day went by that I didn't see it. And she talked about you constantly, bragging about how wonderful you were. That sort of thing was bound to leave a lasting impression."

She brought one hand up to his head, letting her fingers flow through the tumbled waves. "You were married, though, and half a world away. I never consciously let my mind dwell on it. Those deep-seated feelings about you didn't really pop to the surface until I was in the hospital."

"They certainly didn't show up when I was taking your picture," Nicholas said, remembering. "What happened in the hospital?"

"My subconscious blabbed under the anesthesia. And then the doctor tattled on me. There was this shark, you see. Nasty little devil...."

"It would have served me right if he had eaten me," he admitted when she had finished telling him the complicated tale. "Did you really hate me that much?"

"No. But oh, how I tried to!"

"I've been semiacquainted with you for years, too. Melina was so proud of you she used to send me pictures of you cut out of magazines. All the cover-girl shots, and those sexy perfume ads. Her letters were full of news about her best friend, New York's most gorgeous fashion model. I used to look at those pictures and think..." Interspersed with kisses, he told her some of the things he used to think.

"So really we've had each other on our minds for a lot of years," Casi concluded. "But Nicholas, why did you despise me on sight? I could never figure it out. I flew to California all excited about meeting Melina's big brother at last. Yet all you ever said to me was, 'Shut up and smile.'"

He nuzzled her shoulder in apology. "Call it chauvinism. I'd heard too much rah, rah, rah about your success. Then you stepped off that plane, and I knew if I wasn't careful you'd have my scalp to add to your belt. It was either resist you with all my might, or... You were a Career Girl. Capital letters. Tops in your line. And I'd had quite enough of career women to last me a lifetime. Or so I thought."

Shaky ground, Casi warned herself. She continued to mess up his hair with one hand and stroke his shoulder gently with the other, hoping he would decide to tell her about it. Eventually he did.

"My entire marriage could have been described as a career conflict," Nicholas confessed. "Jeanne was extremely competitive, determined to be the best foreign correspondent in the Middle East. When we met in Istanbul there weren't many other Americans in town. We drifted together, thinking we had a lot in common. All we had in common was Istanbul."

He burrowed closer to Casi, warming her with his body heat. "One of us was always in the field. In four years we spent about ten months together. I got sick of the slaughter and the politics over there—sick of everything. I wanted to come home, start a family. Jeanne preferred to head for Beirut, hoping for a Pulitzer Prize. She made arrangements to interview one of the terrorist leaders. I said it was a stupid idea. The argument went on for days. It could have been heard in Ankara. Finally I threw some stuff into a suitcase and said I was through. That that was the end."

"And was it?" Casi asked when the silence had grown uncomfortably long.

"Yeah. A couple of weeks later she walked into an ambush on the way to some camp—an opposition group.... I was a miserable failure as a husband, Casi.

Even if she hadn't died we were heading for a quick divorce. It's bugged me ever since, thinking that maybe if I'd ever really loved her things could have been different."

He dropped a kiss on her forehead. "Anyhow, I came home and began doing other kinds of photography. Then Melina's business got off the ground. She started promoting you as the only model in the world. And the thought of succumbing to that model's gorgeous wiles scared the hell out of me. I bent over backward trying not to like you. What can I say?"

"Say you're sorry you were lousy to me."

"I'm sorry I was lousy to you, Casi." He ruffled her bangs. "The truth is, I couldn't resist you even then. In those last few seconds before the crash I realized that. Casi, I love you. Will you marry me?"

An agonizing pain stabbed through Casi's midsection. She couldn't risk doing that to him, shacklng him for life.... "Nicholas, you mean more to me than anything in the whole world," she moaned. "I'll never, never change my mind about loving you. But...will you ask me again on Saturday? Please?"

"I can't afford to wait that long," Nicholas said gruffly. "By Saturday gossip will have ruined my reputation. I demand that you do the honorable thing—make an honest man out of me." He nibbled at her chin. "You wouldn't want my sister to have to get out grandfather's old shotgun, would you?"

Here was a quixotic switch! Casi burst into a fit of giggles at the notion.

"Cut it out," he grumbled, pressing down on her shoulders to try to make her lie still. She responded by tickling him. Pretty soon he was laughing, too, but the bit of foolishness didn't make him any less persistent.

"I can see you don't think much of my shotgun-wedding idea," he said, pursuing the topic tenaciously. "Neither do I. Actually, what I had in mind was waiting until Melina and Dane come home, bundling them into the car with us and driving up to Reno tonight. It's only about five hours away. They could fly home after the ceremony, and we'd drive back tomorrow. Or Wednesday. Whenever we got out of bed."

"A short but perfect honeymoon! Come on, Nicholas. You don't want to get married like that. All your cousins would be hurt. Besides, you'd want the priest to do it up right."

"Well, of course. With altar boys, a nuptial mass and a choir and all. This is going to be a forever marriage, Casi. The Reno thing is just to hold us until they call out the banns in church." He nudged her gently. "What's the matter? You afraid of living in sin for three weeks?"

No, Casi thought, she was afraid of living in darkness. For herself, but even more for him. She didn't need tea leaves or tarot cards to read his motives in trying to stampede her to the altar. If things didn't turn out well on Friday. . . Nicholas had a tremendous sense of family loyalty and devotion. Look how he'd stayed with Jeanne all those years, in spite of their wretched incompatibility. Married to a blind woman, he wouldn't have the option of chucking things into a suitcase and walking out. Compatible or not, he'd be tied to her forever, bound by chains of duty.

That reason would never be accepted, of course. She tried another argument to account for her delaying tactics.

"More than anything else in the world I want to say yes, Nicholas. But I'm only going to get married once in my whole life, and I want it to be perfect. I won't be led by the hand to stand up in front of some anonymous justice of the peace. Can't you visualize the wedding pictures? I'd look like a fugitive from a Wanted poster!"

A dismal flood of disappointment washed over Nicholas. He had won the championship, but they weren't going to give him the title. Casi was picturing herself as some sort of freak. To him, sighted or not, she was a beautiful, totally desirable woman. She was the wife he wanted. He knew, though, that to keep pushing the subject right now would only cause both of them torment.

"I'll ask you again on Saturday," he capitulated. "The answer had better be yes, Casi. Regardless. Otherwise I'll be the one whose face appears on the Wanted poster. For kidnapping."

He rolled over, yanked the sheet higher around their shoulders and nestled her up against himself. Before they drifted off to sleep they both spent heart-searching moments pondering the implications contained in that word "regardless."

When they awoke they made love again. Quietly, slowly, sweetly this time, giving priority to the fact that Casi's hands wanted to finish looking at Nicholas, the man who had finally convinced her that he loved her, the man she adored. But once again, though it took every ounce of willpower she possessed, she postponed accepting his proposal of marriage.

After he had helped her back into her clothes, Nicholas insisted on feeding her lunch. He made her a milkshake that was half-slush, half-goo. Casi drank it, anyway, and ate what he gave her in spite of the fact that she could picture the scales in her apartment inching up to nudge the red line that bore the warning: DANGER! OVEREATING PAST THIS POINT WILL BE HAZARDOUS TO YOUR FIGURE!

When she had stowed the plates in the dishwasher, they strolled hand in hand out to the barn, where they visited the kittens. Returning through his mother's flower garden, Nicholas picked a bouquet of sweet peas for her and braided some of them through her hair. Then he led her indoors to the comfortable old couch in the kitchen, where they snuggled down to cuddle and kiss and caress and unbutton.

It was a perfectly lovely afternoon. Before they became aware of what time it was, the lights had been on for over an hour in the house up the hill.

"SO THEY'VE GONE BACK TO WORK, and it looks as if everything will continue smoothly from here on in," Melina said, caution balancing relief in her tone. "But I never want to see another arbitrator or lawyer or shop steward again as long as I live. The whole thing was harassment, pure and simple."

"Relax. Your fall line will be out, decorating the backs of half the fashion-conscious women on the coast before the baby arrives," Dane pointed out. "Maybe now you can take the time to appreciate my cooking." He hoisted several cartons of takeout Chinese food in her direction. "Egg roll? Cashew chicken? Sweet 'n sour pork?"

Melina held out her plate. "Some of everything, thank you. And I'll also have time to spend with my husband and brother and my favorite houseguest, thank goodness. Casi, you must be sick of Nicholas's company by now, and I'm thoroughly disgusted with commuting. What say you and I spend all day tomorrow together, doing our hair and nails and talking girl-talk? Let the men tend to business for a change."

Under the circumstances it was hardly possible for Casi to refuse.

"All day? Uh, that sounds wonderful, Melina," she said, dredging up a smile and trying to zap some enthusiasm into her voice. "Nicholas has been a wonderful companion, though. I wouldn't want him to think I didn't appreciate all the time he's taken to teach me things."

"Quit talking about me as if I weren't here," he complained.

"They do that all the time." Dane shook his head sadly. "Make use of us, then cast us aside. Have some more prawns."

"No, I think I'll try a fortune cookie, instead. I've had a question on my mind. Maybe good old Confucius can supply the answer," Nicholas said obliquely. There was a crackle of crisp dough breaking and then the rustle of paper. "'Man who treads wrong path soon winds up at dead end,'" he read out the saying. "So much for any help from that quarter." He pushed back his chair. "Guess it's time I started treading my own path back home. Leave Wednesday open, will you, Casi? I've got some plans in mind for that day."

"Sure."

Had they been alone, she would have asked questions, pried the information out of him if he was reluctant to tell her what it was he had in mind. All things considered, though, she thought it prudent not to risk such an encounter with witnesses present. With her well-known cellophane front she was bound to give something away, and then Melina actually might get out the shotgun.

But after Nicholas left she couldn't get him out of her thoughts. Sitting in the bathtub scrubbing bubbles into her skin, she lifted a foamy hand and found a sweet pea still tangled in her hair. Wrapping a towel around her dripping body, she remembered how marvelous it had felt to be enfolded in Nicholas's arms. Stretching out across the sheet, she wondered if his bed was cold and lonesome, too.

I'd be a good wife to him, she thought fiercely. He'd be so happy with her he'd never want to leave. Regardless.

She loved him utterly, completely. Her heart had found its home. And Nicholas loved her. He wouldn't be human if a few remnants of guilt didn't still linger in his feelings toward her, but he loved her. Together they could overcome anything. Anywhere apart from him would be a dead end.

She stretched out a hand for the radio on her nightstand and turned the little lever. "Are you asleep yet, Nicholas?" she asked softly.

There was a click, followed by a speedy reply. "How can I sleep when my whole body aches from missing you? Are you really going to spend a whole day without me tomorrow?"

"What choice did I have in the matter? It wasn't my idea. I can probably stumble through twenty-four hours on my own." Casi sighed. "I think I can, anyway. But Nicholas, I don't believe I could survive if I had to spend the rest of my life without you. Do you still want to get married?"

There was a loud smack, as though the screen on the other end had just been soundly kissed. "Go haul the others out of bed," Nicholas crowed jubilantly. "I'll be there in five minutes!"

Casi caught her breath, delighted by his enthusiasm. "Calm down, you nut," she said affectionately. "I didn't mean right now. Before we take any vows, you have to know for sure what you're getting yourself into. But if you still want me when the bandages come off, you've got yourself a bride."

"I'll want you for the rest of my life . Nothing's any good without you, Casi. I know that now. Do you swear to me that you won't change your mind? Regardless?"

"Regardless. I couldn't stop thinking about Confucius and his wrong path. Any path away from you would be the wrong one, and—and I don't want to set foot on it. I love you so much, Nicholas."

"You're the only woman in the world for me, Casi. God bless Dane and his fortune cookies! Can I at least come over and make you another milkshake?"

"Go to sleep, darling," she said with a laugh. "Maybe now I can, too."

THE FOLLOWING MORNING encompassed a total of ninety-seven hours. Casi knew. She metered every snail-pace second of it.

Nicholas looked at his watch eighteen times while shaving.

She swallowed a breakfast of French toast and bacon, just to please Melina.

He tossed down half a cup of scalding coffee, burning his tongue. It tasted like battery acid.

Casi helped her hostess with the dishes.

Nicholas tore his disorderly bed apart and remade it with fresh sheets, all the time wishing she were there so they could tear it apart again.

She tried doggedly to keep her mind on the thread of old-time reminiscences flowing past her ears. The details of her life before Nicholas were so vague and unimportant they seemed a part of someone else's existence rather than her own.

He took the horses out for some exercise and lost his way twice on a trail he'd been riding for most of his thirty-six years.

At 12:15 Nicholas stalked into the Jorgensens' house, carrying an enormous flat cardboard box redolent of cheese and spicy sausage. He presented it to his sister with a sheepish grin.

"I decided it would be more fun to come and have my nails done than to stay home alone," he said, jamming his hands in his pockets and rocking back on his heels. "Since I brought the lunch, will you let me join in?"

"Well, for heaven's sake, Nicholas, there's plenty of food in..." Melina's voice dragged to a halt as she looked suspiciously from his beaming countenance to Casi's suddenly radiant face. "Somehow I get the impression that a manicure isn't the main attraction around here. Thanks for the pizza, big brother. Why don't I take a couple of slices out in the backyard and have a picnic by myself?"

"Great idea," Nicholas said approvingly, not even looking at her. "Go ahead and clean the birdbath while you're at it. Plant a few radishes, too."

"Nicholas!" Casi gasped. "This is Melina's house. You shouldn't order her around like that."

"I did mention his tendency toward pushiness, didn't I?" Melina observed casually as she shoveled two triangular slices of mozzarella-topped pizza onto a plate. "Would you guys like some of this? No? Well, I'll be going."

"Hold it, Sis. Casi's right. This is your house. Sit down at the table and enjoy your lunch. I apologize for sabotaging your plans."

"Does that mean you do want some pizza?"

"Uh, no, thanks. I'll just take her." He grabbed Casi's hand and started towing her toward the entry hall.

"Dammit, Nicholas, we were going to do shampoos!" Melina howled behind him.

"Right. I'll see that she gets one."

On that promise Nicholas closed the front door, swept Casi up into his arms and strode down the porch steps with her.

She had never been kidnapped before. It was a thrilling experience. Nevertheless, she managed to put up a token protest just for appearances' sake. "That wasn't nice at all," she scolded. "Can you imagine what she's going to think?"

Nicholas stopped to kiss her, then marched on. "Melina's a very bright girl. Both of us know exactly what she's thinking, and she's right. I told you my reputation would be ruined if you kept putting off the wedding."

"But Nicholas, this really looks terrible. Melina's my friend. I love her."

"She's my sister. I love her, too." He swooped a kiss across her ear. "Pretty soon she'll be your sister, as well. You're going to be living next door to her, visiting back and forth, for at least the next fifty years. She can spare you for one day."

"Two days. You said you had plans for tomorrow," she reminded him. "What are we going to do?"

"Any number of things." Nicholas hugged her tightly. "What do you care? You'll be with me."

"I will," Casi said joyously. "Yes, I will!"

They were at that euphoric stage lovers reach when the world has telescoped into a two-party universe. For the moment, at least, there was nobody else on the planet. The tension was gone. He had proposed; she had accepted. The bedroom was no longer uncharted territory. Casi and Nicholas were free to relax and simply enjoy each other. And they did.

The afternoon alternated between lovemaking, sometimes frenzied, somtimes languorous, and intimate discussions of the subjects of most concern to them.

"I can't remember ever having felt so totally happy," Casi said at one point. She was spread-eagled on top of him, her body molding his, while his hands caressed her satiny buttocks. "That's weird, isn't it? I can't see. Yet I'm gloriously happy simply because I'm with you."

"Not weird, wonderful." It was the first time the topic of her eyesight had been directly broached, although it had been constantly on both their minds for over a month. "Think how you'll feel when you can look straight at me and say, 'I, Casi, take thee, Nicholas...'"

"Knock on wood. If it does work out that way it will be like experiencing an extract of bliss. Pure and undistilled." Her fingers massaged his temples, flirting now and then with his sideburns. "But you know as well as I do there are only six chances out of ten of that happening. Why do you think I tried so hard not to say I'd marry you? I don't want to be a blind albatross dangling around your neck."

Nicholas shivered and clamped her more tightly against himself. "Sweetheart, don't say things like that! You're my lodestar, not my anchor. You've opened up my life, given it a purpose. Just being with you is paradise. This morning taught me a lesson. I don't ever want to be separated from you again, even for a few hours at a time."

Casi propped herself up on one elbow, her hand drifting through his chest hair. "That isn't realistic, you know. For the past couple of weeks we've been almost like Robinson Crusoe and Friday, shipwrecked on a desert island. Don't think I didn't resent it passionately at first, having to follow wherever you led. But there's no way I could have made it through this dark time without your support and guidance."

"You'll always have that, Casi darling."

"And I'm grateful. Still, I've got to stop relying so heavily on you. Yesterday when you were late in showing up I started having a real anxiety attack. That's when I realized it was time I took a few steps on my own again." She kissed his eyelids. "I love being your woman, having you take care of me. But I've got some goals that can't ever be achieved unless I let go of your hand and start acting like a competent adult again."

Although his instincts warred against the notion of relinquishing his role as her protector, Nicholas made an honest effort to understand her need for independence. "What *do* you want most, Casi?" he asked, pulling her face down against his cheek.

Her tongue inscribed warm circles around his ear before she dragged her head backward a few inches, as though to emphasize her point.

"You. For always. That's what I want most. But I want to be a good wife, not a clinging vine. That means turning you loose to go back to being Nicholas the superstar cameraman again rather than my full-time beach-bum companion. And I want your children. I can't be a terrific mother if I'm as dependent on you as one of the babies."

Nicholas exulted silently. It was simply too good to be true. This was all he needed to make his life really complete. "You're not just saying you want children because you know how I feel about family?"

"Nicholas, I literally ache for a baby to love and care for. A few weeks ago I had almost made the decision to pick out some pleasant, comfortable man as a husband just to provide me with the ways and means to that goal."

"You would have settled for someone other than me?" He sounded horrified at the idea.

She dipped her lips toward his mouth. "Darling, I didn't know I was going to *get* you. As far as I knew then, you and I practically hated each other. So, awful as it sounds, yes, I would have settled for compatibility. Chosen someone I liked and done my best to convince him and myself that it was the real thing."

"That doesn't work." Nicholas shook his head. "I tried it once. That kind of marriage can be a real disaster." His arms tightened around her back. "But our marriage is going to be a lifetime grand passion. For you, my love, I will be happy to provide the ways and means toward parenthood."

Casi ruffled his hair. "You're willing to work night and day to get me pregnant?"

"Tirelessly!" Nicholas assured her, and proceeded to demonstrate.

Eventually Casi did get her shampoo. Nicholas not only washed her hair, but dried it afterward, fanning the long, auburn strands out in the warmth of the backyard sun, stroking them gently until they fluffed about his fingers. The process was so enjoyable that Casi wondered how she would ever put up with a beauty parlor again. She hadn't come very far today in asserting her independence, she realized, but at least the subject had been opened for discussion. Little by little they'd work it out. Meanwhile, she thought, as she felt the brush leave her hair and fingers come around to fondle her breast again, it was lovely to be sheltered in his arms.

Melina showed remarkable restraint in curbing her tongue when, long after dinnertime, they finally arrived back at the Jorgensens' house. The next morning, though, when the two women were sitting in the kitchen, she apparently couldn't resist commenting on the situation any longer.

"Have you two set a date yet?" she asked.

Casi choked over a mouthful of steamy black coffee. "That obvious, huh?"

"After yesterday? What a time for my movie camera to be in the closet. I only wish I had pictures of your faces when he said, 'No, thanks. I'll just take her.'"

"If he'd had his way, you and Dane would have been dragged out of bed for a trip to Reno the other night."

Absently Casi traced the raised scrollwork on her mug. "This hasn't been going on the whole time, you know. Up until Monday he was bending over backward to teach me how to cope with life in the dark. Really pushing me to stand on my own two feet again. Then all of a sudden he started carrying me around instead of letting me walk. He's become so protective it's almost unsettling. Does love always affect men that way?"

"Latin men are worse than most when it comes to the macho bit, I'm afraid," Melina murmured. "When they love, they love hard, and they're fiercely possessive. They're all man, and they want the lady of their choice to be all woman. But she never has any doubts about where she stands in his heart."

"Yes. Isn't it glorious?"

"Nicholas's life has been terribly empty for a long time. Right now he's probably overreacting to the fact that he's finally found someone who both needs and loves him." Melina fiddled with her spoon. "I hate to sound like an interfering in-law before you're even married, but if you and Nicholas want to hold on to this wonderful happiness you've found, you should always stop and count to about ninety before you open your mouths. You're both as quick-tempered as the devil, and each of you tends to get your feelings hurt very easily."

"Before, maybe, but not anymore." It was impossible for Casi to visualize herself fighting with Nicholas nowadays.

"That was uncalled-for, I guess, sticking my nose in. It's only that I love you both so much." Melina laughed. "Didn't I tell you Nicholas was something else? I've known it all my life."

"I should have listened to you sooner. I'm so besotted by the man it would be easy to let him go right on petting and pampering me twenty-four hours a day," Casi admitted. She couldn't imagine why Melina sounded so serious. "I've just been a little concerned that he's neglecting his work on account of me. Hopefully, as soon as these wretched bandages come off, we'll be able to start acting a little more rationally."

"Rational or not, it's going to be great having you for a sister-in-law," her friend said warmly. "You're the best thing that's ever happened to my brother."

The discussion came to an abrupt halt when the front door opened. Casi smiled as familiar eager footsteps crossed the entryway tiles. "Good morning," she called. "Come and have some coffee."

"Soledad already made me a whole pot." Nicholas rested his fingertips on her shoulders. "Are you ready to go for a ride?"

Even that light contact had disturbed the regular flutter of Casi's pulse. She reached back and drew his hands forward under her chin, where she could hold them both. "A ride as in sight-seeing?"

Nicholas was trying hard to behave himself in front of his sister. "No, a ride as in visiting Olivia," he replied, thinking of the picnic Soledad had packed, which they would be enjoying a little later. Among other things.

In spite of her trust in him, Casi still felt an unreasonable stab of jealousy whenever she heard Olivia's name mentioned. "Why don't we just go to the beach, instead?" she offered as a counterproposal. "Or better yet, stay here with Melina and get our nails done?"

"Because this is something that's been planned since Sunday and she's expecting us." He hoisted Casi out of the chair. "Up, my love. Where's your jacket? We'll see you later, Melina . . . unless you'd like to come along."

She smiled. "I don't think you two need a chaperon. Besides, I've been putting off doing the laundry. Have a grand time."

Casi sensed that Nicholas had some kind of surprise up his sleeve, so she gave in to the outing gracefully. "Point Reyes isn't very far north of here, is it?" she asked.

"It's only about a half-hour drive to the ranger station." Nicholas waited until they got into the car, then kissed her with loving thoroughness. "Lord, how I missed you! I'll be glad when you're spending every night in my bed, instead of just talking to me over the radio."

"Me, too," Casi murmured. "And if you don't cut that out, we'll be right back in it this morning. Are you sure you want to go visit Olivia?"

"With Soledad running the vacuum, it would be a little hard to concentrate on what I really would like to do," Nicholas said. She could picture his rueful smile. With a reluctance matching her own, he pulled away from her and started the engine.

As they took a shortcut out to connect with the main road, he told her that Point Reyes was a national seashore run by the park service. "Later in the summer we'll come back and visit the lighthouse. Maybe even do some camping on one of the lakes," he promised. "It really is a beautiful place. You'll love it."

"Hmm, maybe. I've never been camping. Do they make sleeping bags built for two?"

Casi's enthusiasm for the trip rose somewhat as they entered the preserve and headed for the Visitors' Center. She rolled down her window, enjoying the fresh, piny scent in the air and listening to the riotous chirping going on overhead.

"You get a symphony with every park visit. Over three hundred varieties of birds make their home here," Nicholas told her.

Olivia came to greet them. Turning her duties over to a fellow ranger, she took Casi's hand as naturally as if they had been friends for a long time. "I'm so glad you could come," she enthused. "I've got something just priceless to show you."

If only the darned girl weren't so genuinely nice it would be easier to go on resenting her, Casi thought. Allowing Olivia to lead her along a carpet-soft path padded with millions of pine needles, she reminded herself that it was only the grandparents who were playing matchmaker. If Nicholas had been seriously interested in Olivia, he would have done something about it a long time ago.

"Here we are," the younger woman said. "This is a little toolshed where we store odds and ends. You'll need to duck your head when we go through the door."

Casi took two steps inside, then stiffened. There was a definite animal odor in the shed, and a lot of agitated yapping was going on in one corner of the small building. She felt Nicholas's hand engulf hers reassuringly.

"Your reaction to Gulliver gave me the idea," he explained. "When Olivia told me about the new litter, I decided that if you met some puppies you might be less afraid of full-grown dogs."

"Well, I appreciate the thought, but—" Casi shivered apprehensively, fighting the urge to turn around and run. "The mother dog isn't here?"

"No, she's having a nap in my room," Olivia assured her. "Do you feel like coming over to meet her family?"

Although she wasn't really in favor of the plan, Casi realized how stupid it would sound if she refused to have anything to do with the puppies after Nicholas and Olivia had gone to all this trouble on her account. Advancing, she steeled herself, determined to make an effort for their sakes. A moment later, a trembling little body with floppy ears and silky-soft hair was placed in her arms. Automatically her hands began to make petting motions. She was quickly rewarded when the puppy nuzzled closer and a slurping tongue lapped at her fingers.

"Oh, my goodness," Casi crooned. "You're just full of affection, aren't you?"

"Cocker spaniels are a very gentle breed. Your worst danger is that he might wet on you. My wash load has doubled in the past couple of weeks," Olivia said with a laugh.

They stayed for about twenty minutes, admiring each of the puppies in turn. By that time Nicholas felt satisfied that Casi's mind was more at ease where baby dogs, at least, were concerned.

He would not have admitted it to anyone, but there was a highly pertinent point to this outing. Friday was coming up fast. Every hour he seemed to grow more fidgety, worrying about the outcome of the bandage removal. He doted on Casi to the point of foolishness, but he was well aware that a person of her independent nature wouldn't be content to let him hold her hand forever. If worse came to worst—and he crossed his fingers that it wouldn't—they could work up to the subject of a guide dog in easy stages.

"The mother must be getting anxious to see her brood again," he said, calling a halt to the pet-nuzzle-slurp cycle at last. "Thanks for taking time out for us, Olivia."

As they left the shed, he turned the subject to a lumber mill in the region whose polluting wastes were causing ecologists no little concern. Olivia mentioned that state inspectors had been alerted and that a couple of stiff letters had already been sent to the mill's management.

"We have several freshwater lakes and a number of streams right here in the park to worry about," she added. "Not to mention all the birds and animals. It could be an ugly mess if they don't find a way to stop the pollution soon."

Casi expressed her own thanks before the ranger returned to her duties. "I'm delighted to hear you talking about the environment again," she told Nicholas as they headed back to the car. "Are lumber mills going to be the topic of your new book?"

"They're not the prime focus, but they will be included. All of us are worried about the contaminants pouring into our rivers and lakes and finding their way out to sea." He hugged her close to him. "I want this to be a good world for our children to grow up in, Casi. Here in the West we've already taken a lot of steps to clean up the air. And the plight of Lake Tahoe has called dramatic attention to the water, as well. It's about time!"

"That's wonderful," she said. "And so were the puppies, incidentally, though I definitely prefer your kittens. What now, coach?"

"Want to come down to the shore and find a nice spot for a picnic? There are lots of interesting tide pools on this stretch of the coast." Driving along the winding route, he explained that on summer weekends shuttle buses were used to take visitors to the lighthouse and Drake's Beach, but he and Casi had been given permission to use their own car.

It was a pleasantly varied day, divided between walks and kisses, tide-pooling and hugs, picnics and caresses. At about three o'clock the wind came up, and Casi was glad Nicholas had thought to bring along jackets. "That breeze has a bite to it," she said, shrugging into hers.

"We could go bundle in the car," Nicholas suggested.

"Umm. Or go home to one of the houses. Which would you prefer?"

"Soledad and her vacuum will be long gone," he said decisively.

Remembering her remarks about feeling disoriented during the drive from the hospital, Nicholas took pains to see that she didn't get out of touch with her surroundings here. He described the different areas of the park they were passing through, told her when to wave as they passed the rangers' gate and let her know when they turned onto the main road.

For a fleeting moment he thought of Friday. He prayed that after that day he could bring her back to see it all for herself.

Snuggling close to him, Casi lost herself in the enjoyment of his company. Once again he used the shortcut, slowing down on the winter-rutted, one-lane road circling through the Penheiro property.

"Dane's not home yet," he commented, sending a glance toward the Jorgensens' driveway. "But . . ."

"What's the matter?" Casi caught the apprehensive note in his voice before it trailed off.

"Probably nothing. There's a Sheriff's car in front of my house," Nicholas answered, accelerating a bit. "It's one of the sheriff's deputies. I know him pretty well." He braked to a halt. "Stay here, sweetheart, and let me find out what this is all about."

Dear Lord, don't let anything have happened to Dane! Casi's lips moved in silent entreaty as she thought of the snaking highway Melina's husband had to travel every day. Obediently she sat still for a minute. Then, unable to bear the suspense, she opened the car door and started walking slowly downhill. Nicholas's voice, pitched low, mixed with the rumble of another masculine baritone. She caught the word "litigation," then the phrase, "I'm really sorry, pal."

"What is it?" Casi called, taking a few more steps in their direction. "Is anything wrong?"

There was something both angry and wretched about the thud of the footsteps that crunched toward her.

"Wrong?" Nicholas asked. The word sounded chewed, mangled, as though it had been squeezed out between clenched teeth. "I guess that depends on your point of view. When did you decide to sue me, Casi?"

9

CASI'S MOUTH DROPPED OPEN. The question had hit her like a slap in the face. "What did you say?" she gasped.

"You heard me. Don't bother with the act, Casi. I know all about the lawsuit." Nicholas's words rasped at her, each one acting like the jagged point of the spur, roweling into her flesh.

"You—you know about the lawsuit?" she repeated, sounding to her own ears like a particularly dim-witted parrot.

Nicholas blazed on, his voice trembling with scorn, not giving her a chance to recover her equilibrium.

"Sheriff Mandville and I were classmates. You hadn't bargained on someone who knew me well spilling the beans so soon, had you? Better tell your lawyer his timing was off by several days. I'm sure I wasn't meant to receive the summons until after you had left Melina's house permanently."

"But I wouldn't—"

She heard the spurt of gravel splattering against dirt, as though his toe had gouged angrily into the ground and sent pebbles flying like a swarm of agitated bees. "I guess now we both know why you were so reluctant to accept my sister's hospitality," he taunted bitterly. "Anybody with even half a conscience would have felt the same way. Talk about biting the hand that feeds you!"

He doesn't mean it, she thought dizzily. *He can't be saying those things to me!*

Swaying under the force of his verbal assault, Casi felt a moment's regret that she had not remained in the car. She desperately needed something solid to cling to. Clenching her fists, she dug her nails deliberately into her palms so that the sharp little circlets of pain would keep her conscious. It would be the final indignity to pass out here, in front of this man whose love seemed to have suddenly turned to hate.

In the few seconds' breathing space she was allowed, she made an effort to understand what was going on. Someone had filed a lawsuit against Nicholas. That much, at least, penetrated the haze of distressed foreboding clouding her brain and seeping through her entire body. The news brought by the deputy had obviously been a terrible blow to Nicholas. Shock was evident in every word he spoke.

But why was he lashing out at her, instead of clinging to her for comfort?

With a valiant effort Casi kept her chin from wobbling. The plea that spilled from her lips trembled, instead, begging him to stop this unjust punishment.

"Nicholas, won't you please calm down? Think about what you're saying. I don't deserve—"

"You don't 'deserve'!" His laugh was short and brutal.

"I did nothing to merit any of this," she insisted, bleeding inside. "Tell me what's happened that you should turn against me so viciously."

"You want it spelled out in words of one syllable?" he asked scathingly. "Okay, then, hear this. I have just been informed that there is a summons headed my way. The paperwork is on its way over from San Francisco by special courier. My friends in the Sheriff's Depart-

ment thought I would appreciate having a few hours'
advance notice. They figured it might take me a while
to adjust to the fact that I'm being sued for half a million dollars because of the ferryboat incident."

"Half a—" It was an incomprenhensible sum. "And
you asked *me* when I—"

"That's right. When. When did you decide to sue me,
Casi?" The question was tight, choked, riddled with
pain. Risking the deepest wound of all, he forced himself to continue. "It would make a difference, you
know. I'd like to believe you made the decision before
you left the hospital. Before we—"

"I didn't! Not then, not ever!"

Her entire being was chilled by the frigid sarcasm of
his words. There was no longer any loving warmth in
Nicholas's tone, only anguish and hostility. Freezing
from the inside out, she shrugged down into the folds
of her fleecy jacket, wishing it could protect her,
knowing it could not. Nothing could.

Keeping her face rigid, she asked what she had to ask.
"How could you even think that I would do such a thing
to you?"

"You told me yourself, Casi. Don't you remember
what you said?"

His verbal assault was like standing in the middle of
a New York storm feeling chips of ice prod into her skin.
Each syllable was gouging, lacerating.

"Two weeks ago, the day the strike hit Melina's studio, we did a little necking in your bedroom. I thanked
you for the therapy. You said, 'Wait till you get my bill.'
Well, it's here, Casi. Your invoice has finally been de-
livered."

She did remember that silly, offhanded remark. But
how insulting for him to think . . .

"The bill I referred to that day was meant to be payable in hugs and kisses. I've already collected on it." Casi was so stunned by his lack of faith in her that she had to bite her tongue to keep the last words from ending with a sob. She swallowed hard. "But I don't suppose you would believe that any more than you'd believe anything else I've tried to say in my own defense. Did your good buddy tell you that I'm the Mata Hari who stabbed you with this lawsuit?"

The tight, pinched, colorless-as-a-marble-statue look on her face combined with the agony in her tone penetrated Nicholas's emotion-clogged consciousness at last. His tormented dark gaze fastened on the woman he had so adored. All the scorn and fury drained away, leaving only a residual ache. From underneath Casi's bandage salty rivulets had begun furrowing down her cheeks. He blinked back a smarting at the corners of his own eyes.

"Yes," he said hoarsely. "At least he assumed . . ."

"'Assumed'? You've condemned me on the basis of an assumption? Salem's witches got a fairer trial before they went to the stake, Nicholas!"

It was a protestation of innocence, and no one knew better than he that Casi wasn't capable of telling a believable lie. But without her involvement none of this made sense.

"Casi," he whispered, glad that she couldn't see the anguish on his face. "No one else would have had any possible reason . . ."

Had he slapped her it would have done less harm. Pride stiffened her spine.

"'No one else.' So I'm elected." The words shuddered out unsteadily. Another instant and she knew she would break into a thousand pieces. Already her breathing was so distressed that her words came in gasps. Tears slid from under the bandage. She felt feverish, as though a virus were blazing its hot, fuzzy way through her head while a chill shivered its way through the rest of her tall frame.

Up ahead a car door slammed. She clutched at the sound like a lifeline and took two strides forward, away from Nicholas.

"We're not finished yet. Don't walk away from me, Casi!"

The words were a plea as well as an order, doubt having quivered its way into the inflection. She knew every cadence of his speech. Hadn't she spent weeks listening with all her heart and soul? His first white-hot fury had melted and become diluted with uncertainty. Yet at first he'd had no doubt at all about her guilt. His accusations had struck out blindly, as blindly as she was now staggering downhill.

"Casi!" he roared. Running thuds kicked up the gravel alongside her. "Where the hell do you think you're going?"

She jerked to a standstill, arrested in flight by the iron grip that had closed over her slender arm. Swinging around to confront him, she flailed at his wrist with her free hand, struggling to break clear.

"Let go of me!" she demanded. "You can stand in the middle of this road for the rest of your life, but I won't stay here and listen to you any longer. You've had your say. Save the rest of it for the courtroom!"

"We're going to get this straightened out!"

"That's hilarious coming from you, Nicholas. You can't have forgotten so soon. You already have me pegged me as the guilty party."

"There wasn't anybody else!" His words jerked out, anguished spurts of sound that made Casi's ears sorrow at having to listen to them. "You were the one who was hurt!"

"Not the way I'm hurt now," she moaned, shaking free of his restraining grip and stumbling toward the car she knew couldn't be far ahead. "Officer," she called, waving to flag him down as an engine roared to life. "Wait a minute!"

Nicholas hadn't tried to grab her again, but he was keeping pace. "Casi, if you'll just calm down and listen to me—"

"Is anything wrong?" The deputy's deep voice cut through the agitated pleading.

Casi raised her voice to answer him. "Yes, I'm going to need a ride. Hold it one second, will you?" She swung back to Nicholas. "Why should I listen? You've said too much already. It's going to take me the rest of my life to get over the fact that the man who claimed to love me doesn't trust me. Goodbye, Nicholas!"

"'A ride'?" Sounding befuddled, the deputy had advanced a few paces.

"Yes." Casi tightened her voice with steely control. "I'm in a hurry, and as you may have noticed, I have trouble seeing where I'm going. Would you give me a lift, please, to the next house up the hill?"

"Well . . . sure." He darted a swift look at Nicholas, then another at her agonized expression. "Be glad to."

The next instant he was assisting her into the front seat. Casi sat rigidly, head high, hands clenched in her lap as the vehicle made a wide sweep around the other car still blocking the middle of the road. Ruts grabbed the wheels, jolting her. A minute or two later he pulled up with a jerk.

"Here's the Jorgensens' house. This where you wanted to go? I'll be glad to help you inside."

"That won't be necessary, thank you." Casi swung open the car door. "I appreciate the transportation."

Counting silently, she strode up the gravel path, mounted the steps and entered the house. From the kitchen she could hear canned laughter, then the "come on and buy, folks" snake oil of a TV salesman. A chair scraped and bare feet padded forward to investigate the closing of the front door.

"Oh, hi," Melina said. "Gee, you're back early. I didn't expect . . ." Her voice trailed off. Casi knew that her transparently anguished expression was being read and comprehended. "Something's wrong, isn't it? Did you guys have a fight? Where's Nicholas?"

"Yes, yes, and somewhere down the road." Casi dropped into a chair and pressed her fingers to her temples. She could still hardly take in what had happened. How he could have suspected for one minute that she would . . . The swift, devastating betrayal of that accusation was almost impossible to comprehend. One minute they had been laughing, holding hands, and the next . . . finished.

"Want to have some iced tea and talk it over?" Melina asked quietly.

Casi shook her head. "I couldn't swallow anything right now." Her throat felt raw, her chest painful, as though some monumental weight were pressing all the air out of her lungs. Her hands began to shake; she could feel moisture prickling at the folds of the bandage. "I—excuse me, Melina, I really need to be alone."

Getting up unsteadily, she wheeled toward the bedroom wing before the wracking sobs she knew were coming could explode outward. With the door closed, she hurled across the bed and shoved the pillow underneath her face to muffle the sounds of weeping. The torrent gushed on and on. Rather than bringing relief, the tears only intensified her distress and brought fresh waves of sorrow washing over her. Her shoulders heaved in utter misery. All that wonderful newfound happiness, all their bright plans, gone. Forever.

What he had done was unforgivable! Olivia could have him. The shark could have him! Nothing would be the same again.

By the time she finally lifted her head off the sodden pillow she felt totally drained, so weary she could hardly move. It was a temptation just to curl up, let the blessed void of sleep flood over her as the tears had done. Casi resisted. She fumbled in the medicine cabinet for aspirin, swallowed three of them in hopes of easing the pain in her throat, then splashed cold water on her face, bandage and all. What did it matter? Her face could hardly get any wetter.

Heading back into the bedroom, Casi stalked to the closet and hoisted out her suitcase. Trying to remember what clothes she had brought with her all those weeks ago, she started ripping things off hangers and bundling them inside the case. Then she turned to the nightstand, emptying it except for the change of lingerie left to wear in the morning along with the lightweight wool dress and low-heeled shoes she had set aside earlier.

Snapping the latches, she started to lift the suitcase off the bed. A soft tap at the door interrupted her.

"Casi, may I come in?" Melina asked.

She turned toward the sound of her friend's voice. "Of course. I was just tidying up."

"You—you look as if you had a good cry. Sometimes that helps get the rage out of your system. I'm sure it must have been rage. When Nicholas told me what happened I felt like killing him myself."

"Be my guest," Casi said cryptically.

Melina ignored the twisted invitation. "He's here, Casi," she said. "Nicholas sent me to ask if you would allow him to come in and throw himself on your mercy."

Casi turned her face away. "Why would he want to do that?"

"Because he knows now how terribly wrong he was, how dreadfully he misjudged you. Oh, Casi, my brother loves you so much. We all do."

"But he had to wait for the summons to arrive before he'd take my word that I was innocent, didn't he?" Casi said bitterly. "He wouldn't believe . . ." She took a jagged breath. "Was the plaintiff named on the document?"

"Yes. The two moonlighters from the electrician's union who worked on the lights that night brought the suit. They're seeking damages for mental anguish and a few days' lost work time. The case has been given an early place on the docket because of all the newspaper publicity that the accident generated."

"I always would have wondered who I took the blame for," Casi said, determined that she wasn't going to break down again. "Well, I guess now that the mystery is solved, we can all start picking up our lives where they left off before."

But for her there wasn't anything to pick up, she thought. What had happened prior to her falling in love with Nicholas belonged to another world, another person. All she had left was her future. And her dignity, though she wouldn't even have that if Melina didn't get out of here soon. They knew each other too well.

"Don't do this. To him or to yourself," Melina was pleading. "Nicholas knows what a fool he's been. Won't

you let him come tell you himself how badly he wants
to make things right between you again?"

"That really isn't possible, Melina. You didn't hear
him out there in the road. He said...all sorts of things."
Her throat closed for a moment. She took a shaky
breath and added, "Tell him I wish him luck with the
moonlighters, will you?"

"You're as stubborn as my idiot brother!"

"Well, you did warn me. Incidentally, it's nice of you
not to say, 'I told you so.' You certainly have every
right." She gestured toward her packed suitcase. "Ask
Dane to call me when he gets up in the morning, will
you, please? I'd like to ride into town with him tomorrow."

"To ... the hospital?"

"Where else have I got to go?"

"There isn't any chance—"

"No," Casi said. "There isn't any chance at all."

Later, lying in the silent room, she tried to will herself to sleep. Perversely, drowsiness had now become
elusive. For what seemed like hours she lay there, tossing from side to side, yearning helplessly for oblivion
to come and blot out her pain. Suddenly, out of the
stillness, there was a click of static and she heard her
name being spoken.

"Casi?" Nicholas said over the radio. "Can you hear
me?"

I listened to you once too often, she thought, not
moving.

"My behavior was beneath contempt. I know that,"
he went on. "It just hurt so bad when I thought you
had—I must have been out of my mind. I wanted to say
I'm sorry, that's all. For what it's worth, Casi, I'm
sorry."

In the wretched silence that followed she heard his constricted breathing. "Won't you please say something?" Nicholas pleaded. "Scream at me, call me names if you want. Just talk to me. I'm begging you, Casi, on my knees. Don't shut me out of your life, sweetheart. I love you so much...."

His tone of utter misery clawed at her heart. Every word was another wound, another wrenching, twisting reminder of the happiness they had known together.

With a grieving sob Casi flung back the covers. *I can't stand this,* she thought desperately. *I'll lose my mind if I have to hear any more!*

Groping unsteadily toward the nightstand, she closed her fingers over the plastic case and squeezed both palms around it, muffling his voice. Weaving like a drunk, she made it into the bathroom and dropped the radio with a thud into the nearly empty hamper. Grabbing towels, she stuffed them in on top of it. Their damp, heavy bulk muted the sounds it continued to make, and the slamming of the lid choked off the last vestiges of his pleading words. For good measure, she shut the bathroom door before fleeing back to bed.

A new storm of weeping flooded over her there. Wave after bitter wave of salty tears gushed down her cheeks. She had effectively shut his voice out of her ears, but in her brain it went on and on, mingling with the cruel accusations he had flung at her that afternoon.

"I DON'T THINK the vacation did you any good," Annabelle observed bluntly. "You're looking just as peaked as when you left here."

"It's been a long three weeks," Casi snapped. "When will Dr. Harvey be able to see me?"

"He has you on the agenda for tomorrow at nine o'clock. You're a sucker for punishment, you know, coming to this place a whole day early."

Casi sighed heavily. "Go away, Annabelle, and come back with a sleeping pill, will you? I'm trying to forget just what a sucker I *have* been!"

Even with the aid of medication she had trouble composing her mind enough to allow sleep to come. Fears about the upcoming ordeal intensified with the passing of each interminable hour bringing the time for the unveiling of her eyes ever closer. And the agony caused by Nicholas's brutal assumption that she would have stabbed him in the back with a lawsuit grew even sharper as her brain continued to take in the enormity of her loss.

If only she could hate him, despise him, as she knew she should. But she wasn't capable of such feelings toward Nicholas. He had been friend, teacher, companion, lover. There was not another man like him on the face of the earth. For the rest of her life, Casi knew, she would be helplessly, hopelessly in love with him.

She regretted now ever having allowed herself to be talked into leaving the hospital for that fateful three-week period. The poet who wrote that it was better to have loved and lost than never to have loved at all knew very little about heartbreak. It would have been much more helpful to her in the long run if she had stayed on in the city and used this time of waiting to try to formulate some new career plans.

With a pang Casi realized that her past, all of it, was now a closed book. The glamorous way of life in front of the cameras that had brought her fame and fortune was over. So, too, were her dreams of a happy, loving marriage to Nicholas.

Although at first it seemed that she possessed no other skills to offer the world, she now began to consider the possiblility of using her own former success in modeling to help guide other young aspirants to the top of that profession. She had learned the tricks of the trade the hard way, by trial and error. Lying in the rigid hospital bed, trying not to think of what would happen if the bandages came off and darkness remained, she doggedly began formulating a way in which her own experiences could be used to guide the budding careers of those who hoped to follow in her footsteps.

The drastic changeover from doer to teacher would be far from easy. She hoped there would be some satisfaction, some pride to be found in the new occupation. There would have to be, Casi warned herself bitterly. It was all she was ever going to have.

Cold sweat trickled off Casi's brow, dappled her upper lip. Over and over she had repeated all the prayers she'd been taught as a child, and added numerous ad-lib appeals to heaven that poured directly from her heart. Trapped in her prison of darkness, she could hear the accelerated pace of the hospital as the morning dragged by: carts trundling up and down the halls, voices mingling at the nurses' station as the shift changed. Shortly afterward the odor of food assailed her senses, increasing her nausea, her trepidation. Soon she would know.

Turning the tiny abalone shell over and over in her hands, she thought what a difference it would have made if Nicholas could have been here to see her through this last-minute horror, how his voice would have soothed her, his touch comforted her. She had found the little shell in the pocket of her jacket as she was being driven across the bridge yesterday morning. It was the one and only reminder of him and their days together that she had carried away with her. The memories it inspired as she traced her fingers across it were so poignant that she could feel tears welling up again. Yet she couldn't bring herself to lay it aside.

Casi was still clutching it when the door opened and limping footsteps approached. Terror tied knots in her throat. She stuttered out a greeting. "Are you ready to—to get it over with?"

"I am if you are," Dr. Harvey replied. "Let's see what we have here."

Competent hands touched her face. Adhesive tape was peeled back, cotton lifted away. Casi realized she was holding her breath. She tried to let it go, made an effort to breathe normally, but the tremors rocking her body made respiration difficult.

The final layer of padding was removed. Some of the gloom seemed to lighten. Maybe that was wishful thinking, though. She gasped as a moist swab outlined her eyelids, separating the matted lashes.

"Try it," the doctor ordered. "Open them up, Casi."

She forced a shuddery whisper past her lips. "You sound as scared as me."

Shaking so hard the bed seemed to zigzag beneath her, she dragged at the heavy lids. The sharp edge of the abalone cut into her palm, but Casi didn't notice the pain. She winced as light penetrated the long-disused irises. The dizziness of relief washed over her as a fuzzy form wavered before her eyes.

"Say something, for God's sake!" A betraying tremble of fear shook his voice.

"Yes!" Casi sobbed. "Yes, you're there! I can see you!"

It was another hour before the foggy images she had perceived upon first opening her eyes tightened into firm shapes and forms. They took it little by little, with Annabelle letting first one slit of light, then a second in through the Venetian blinds. Casi cringed against the pillow as the glare of the ophthalmologist's flashlight beamed across her eyes for a quick inspection.

"You're going to be fine," Dr. Harvey said with a sigh, his voice weak with relief. "I was praying you wouldn't let me down."

"It's—it's over, then?"

"Just about. I want to run a battery of tests this afternoon, but from what I can observe now, your vision should be almost as good as new. Here." He handed her a pair of dark glasses. "You'll need to keep these on for a few days until your eyes become more accustomed to the light."

"You had a lot of faith to bring these along," she said shakily. "Thank you."

When he had gone she got out of bed and walked on unsteady legs into the small adjacent bathroom, knowing she would never be able to rest until she'd had a look in the mirror. The face that stared back at her from the glass was thin, ashen with strain. Casi leaned closer. A dozen tiny white lines crisscrossed the area around her eyes and forehead, but they weren't terribly noticeable. Staring into the green depths of her eyes, she could perceive no evidence of the complicated laser surgery that had restored her vision.

The lab tests reinforced Dr. Harvey's confidence that there would be no serious aftereffects from the damage her eyes had sustained. "It's a miracle," he said at last. "I'm proud of you, Casi. Proud of me, too. Together we did a good job of putting things back together. Have you told your friends the good news yet?"

"No. I'll give them a call," she said with deliberate vagueness. "It's all right if I go home now, isn't it? I can get on a plane without any ill effects?"

"Can't wait to bid California goodbye, huh?" He nodded. "Sure, book your flight. Since it's past noon you might as well spend one last night with us and check out in the morning. It'll save you transferring to a hotel. You'll be charged for today in any event."

Casi brought her head up sharply. "My God, the bill! I never gave it a moment's thought. It must be astronomical. I'd better go to the office and start filling out insurance papers!"

The hospital accountant looked up from the readout on the computer screen she had checked in response to Casi's inquiry. "The previous charges have already been take care of, Miss Cavanaugh."

"I don't understand." Casi stared at the woman in bewilderment. "I'm sure I would have remembered signing the forms. Did you get a blanket approval from my insurance company?"

The accountent punched a few keys, seeking additional information from the computer. "It wasn't an insurance payment. The account was settled by a Mr. Nicholas Penheiro. He gave us a personal check for the full amount."

"What—what was the total?"

The answer left her reeling. The charges added up to more than most people made in an entire year!

"He'll have to be reimbursed," Casi said weakly. "My coverage is comprehensive." She fumbled in her wallet for the card of her health-insurance carrier, then pushed it across the counter. "If you don't mind, I'm going to need your help with the paperwork."

An hour later she turned away from the window in exhaustion, having made arrangements for not only the hospital charges but Dr. Harvey's fee and the ambulance bill to be submitted to her insurance company. Even if she'd had any desire for revenge against Nicholas, she could not allow him to assume the tremendous burden of her medical expenses. The hospital bill alone would have been enough to bankrupt most people. And now with that lawsuit coming up... She shuddered at the thought of the half-million dollars the electricians were demanding. Nicholas couldn't possibly pay it, not without selling his land—the land his grandfather had scrimped and saved for years to acquire.

"Miss Cavanaugh?"

Casi wheeled to face the short, bald-headed man who had suddenly appeared at her elbow. "Yes?"

"I have a subpoena for you," he said brusquely, fishing a sheet of paper out of the depths of his tweed overcoat. "You will be required to appear in court this coming Tuesday in the case of Dalmott and Victor vs. Penheiro."

She could only blink at him through the shield of her dark glasses as her hand automatically closed over the folded paper he held out. "In...court?"

"Yes, ma'am. You're being called as a witness for the prosecution." He spun on his heel and strode away before she could reply.

Casi tottered to the nearest chair and sank onto it. With trembling fingers she opened the long white sheet that was covered with black, very official-looking printing. A witness for the prosecution, she thought in shock. She would be forced to sit there with Nicholas's accusers, required to testify against him.

The experience was bound to destroy any last shred of feeling he had for her!

It took a long time to steel herself to make the phone call. Her dinner tray had arrived and been carried off untouched before she found the courage to dial the Jorgensens' number.

The receiver was snatched up on the other end at the first ring of the bell. Hearing Melina's breathless response, Casi knew that she must have been poised nearby, waiting for news.

"Hi, it's me," she said. "I didn't want to call you until the doctor had run all the tests, made sure it was going to last. It—it's all right. I can see."

"Oh, thank God!" There was garbled intermission while Melina relayed the wonderful news to Dane. "We're both just dancing with excitement for you," she bubbled, coming back on the line. "You must be ecstatic with joy!"

"If you only knew! I had been terrified of letting myself hope too hard, but that ordeal is finally over." Casi gulped emotionally. "Pass the word on down the hill, would you? Tell him—tell him he doesn't need to worry about me anymore."

"I had so hoped—Casi, won't you change your mind and at least talk to Nicholas yourself? I *know* you love him."

"That's beside the point." Unable to deny the truth, she grabbed for a tissue. Now for the bad news. "There's something else, something awful I've got to tell you," she said. "I was handed a subpeona today. They're going to make me go into court and testify for the prosecution."

"Dear Lord, what next!"

"I don't think things could possibly get any worse." Casi groaned into the receiver. "Obviously they planned the timing to coincide with my release from the hospital. They intend to use me to hurt him, and—and there isn't anything I can do to stop them."

She took a deep breath to try to put some courage back into her voice. "Just let him know it wasn't my idea, okay, Melina? Maybe he'll believe you."

10

"Do you swear to tell the truth, the whole truth and nothing but the truth, so help you God?"

"I do."

"Please be seated."

Casi took her chair in the witness box and let her eyes roam within a tightly restricted radius around the chamber, taking in the rugged stone walls, the flags draped ceremoniously from their poles, the solemn face of the bailiff who had just taken her oath. She was slowly becoming accustomed to looking at things again, but she knew it was one activity she would never tire of. In the past four days she had filled her eyes greedily each time they opened, cramming them full of color, light, reflections, nature's bounty—all the beauty of life she had missed so dreadfully during what she had come to think of as her dark time.

Ever since entering the courtroom she had steadfastly avoided glancing toward the tall, black-haired man who, in the company of his own lawyer, sat at the front table on one side of the room. Her face was about as skilled at concealment as a traffic signal. If she so much as rested her eyes on him for a single moment, her countenance would start mirroring all the hurt and anguish he had recently caused her. Worse yet, the deeply abiding love she still felt for him would inevitably shine forth from her emerald eyes. A clever attorney would have no trouble diagnosing and using those rampaging emotions to strike at Nicholas through her.

Concentrating intently on keeping her features immobile, Casi fastened her gaze on the man who had risen to interrogate her. His voice had a surface geniality as he drew from her several ordinary facts about her age, occupation and place of residence. Yet those cold, gray eyes were deadly. They warned her that she dared not drop her guard for an instant. Already, because of her refusal to discuss her testimony with him in advance, he was regarding her as a hostile witness. Now, as he got to the point of her presence on the stand, he began to probe more deeply, seeking a way to expose her vulnerability.

"Miss Cavanaugh, would you tell the court exactly why you and a number of other people embarked on a ferryboat excursion on the evening of last February nineteenth?"

"We were there for a photography session. The purpose was to take publicity pictures of a new line of fashions."

"Wasn't this quite an unusual locale?"

Casi sensed a trap. Without a doubt those electricians had overheard some of the arguments she and Nicholas had had about the wisdom of utilizing that creaky old vessel.

"No more unusual than many others," she replied impartially. "I've modeled clothing standing on everything from water skis to the steps of an Egyptian pyramid. Exotic backgrounds add to the appeal of the item advertised."

That wasn't what he had wanted to hear. His eyes narrowed, and he advanced a step. "The photographer was the defendant in this case, Mr. Nicholas Penheiro?"

"Yes."

"And your relationship to him?" he asked silkily.

"I was the image in his lens."

"I beg your pardon?"

Maintaining a semblance of poise, Casi spread her long, tapering fingers in a wide gesture. "I modeled the fashions the designer created. The cameraman looked through his range finder and took my picture. That was our relationship."

"Highly professional, in other words."

"Completely."

"Was his attitude equally professional where the electricians were concerned?"

Casi tilted her chin defiantly. "Mr. Penheiro was there to take photographs. The electricians were being well paid to position the lights. Everyone had a job to do."

"In the course of performing that 'job,' as you call it, Mr. Penheiro didn't shout at the workmen? Didn't browbeat them into using shortcuts, into overlooking certain safety precautions?"

"During the six days I worked with the crew on that assignment I never once heard Mr. Penheiro shout," she replied, choosing her words carefully.

"But it was he who gave the orders?"

"Yes."

"So if the lights were poorly installed or insufficient care was taken with their placement, this was done in accordance with the defendant's instructions?"

In abject misery, Casi wished she were allowed to stand and face her tormentor. He might not be so quick to harass her if he had to stare up at her, towering several inches over his head.

"Please answer the question!"

"The electricians were supposed to know how to install the lights," she said faintly.

"Nevertheless Mr. Penheiro told them what he wanted done?"

"I—yes, I think so."

"He was fully responsible for their arrangement?" the steely voice persisted.

"As far as I know, yes."

Please, Nicholas, don't hate me, Casi prayed as the admission was dragged from her.

"All right, Miss Cavanaugh, now that we have established the fact that Mr. Penheiro was totally in charge of this operation, perhaps you'll be good enough to tell us exactly what happened that night."

Determined to stick to the truth but say no more than was absolutely necessary, Casi struggled to keep her summary as succinct as possible.

"We left the pier at about five in the afternoon and sailed a short distance out on the bay. It took a long time to set up the lighting. I ramained at the stern of the boat while that was being attended to. When Mr. Penheiro signaled that he was ready to begin, I came down to the bow and assumed my position at the railing. After I had been posing for a couple of minutes, I heard a voice yell a warning for me to look out. I threw up a hand and started to run, and—and that's all I remember."

"Before you took your place at the railing you don't recall tripping over a coil of extension cords?"

"I stepped over them."

"Realizing they were dangerous."

"Realizing that they were on the deck, I stepped over them."

Casi felt an icy dread each time this man looked at her. He was an implacable foe, a wily adversary, and what his skill with words could do to Nicholas didn't bear thinking about. Already he had forced admissions from her that were dreadfully harmful to the man she loved. What was he going to ask next? She tightened her muscles isometrically, trying to quell the tremors racing up her spine, and waited for his renewed assault.

"Those cords were in fact extremely hazardous, were they not? Because in spite of having ordered them to be dropped in that exact position, Mr. Penheiro himself caught his ankle in them and caused the overhead light to topple. Isn't that what happened, Miss Cavanaugh?"

"All those lights were in my eyes," she protested. "I couldn't see what was happening."

"When the spotlight fell there was a thunderous crash and an explosion of glass. That didn't leave an indelible impression on your mind?"

Casi shrank from him. "No," she whispered. "I lost consciousness."

"Why?"

"I—I was injured."

"Seriously injured?"

"Yes. I can't tell you any more—"

"So seriously injured, in fact, that you had extensive eye surgery that same night. A laser beam had to be employed to remove the glass particles. You were slashed in dozens of places by the flying glass. You lost your vision for a period of nearly six weeks, is that not so?"

"I got it back!" Casi cried.

"That is indeed wonderful news." The attorney's voice was tinged with sarcasm. "We're all delighted that your vision has been restored. You'll be returning to your highly paid occupation as a fashion model, I take it?"

Here it comes, Casi thought with a sinking sensation of rock-bottom despair. The one thing that she had concealed from Nicholas. She wished he didn't have to find out this way, wished she had told him before.

"I haven't decided what I'll be doing when I return to New York," she fenced, hoping to forestall further questions on the subject.

"In any event you will no longer be employed as a fashion model, will you?"

"I . . . don't think so."

"Because your eyes would be unable to tolerate the glaring lights and flashbulbs, is that not so, Miss Cavanaugh? Isn't it true that you will never be able to resume your former lucrative occupation because to do so would be to risk permanent blindness?"

Over his shoulder Casi caught a sudden jerk of movement from the front table. Nicholas had reacted as though he'd been shot. The knowledge of how that brutal revelation must have jolted him infused her entire being with anger. They had no right to do this to her. Using her as a club to beat him into the ground!

Her fury gave her the courage to counterattack.

"You've got it right," she said icily. "I was badly hurt, and now I've lost my job. But you seem to forget that I'm not the one who brought this lawsuit into court, Mr. Hopkins. Were your clients also seriously injured? Or did they merely view the accident as an easy way to collect a huge sum of money? Is that what you call justice around here?"

Sputtering in rage, the prosecuting attorney managed to have her last remarks stricken from the record, but Casi had made her point. She saw the judge regarding her thoughtfully as she was excused to step down. Holding her head high, looking neither left nor right, she marched down the aisle and took a seat in the rear of the courtroom.

Nicholas buried his face in his hands. She must have known, he thought. Weeks ago. But she had kept the knowledge to herself. Even when he was hurling unjust accusations at her, she had never taunted him with the fact that because of him her career was finished forever.

From the moment she had entered the room he hadn't been able to take his eyes off her. In the full-skirted, café-au-lait-colored suit and the white blouse with its frilly ruffles curling around her throat she was the very essence of desirable femininity. But no more so than when she had worn jeans and a thick sweatshirt, even with the blindfold covering her beautiful emerald eyes. Nicholas's heart wrenched in sorrow. Both in actions and in words he had damaged her irreparably. Yet, though she hadn't once glanced in his direction, she had fought for him up there. Every admission of his guilt was dragged unwillingly from her lips; she had tried with all her loyalty to defend him.

Were it not for his imbecilic stupidity she would have been his wife by now. Suddenly it didn't matter to Nicholas whether the lawsuit went against him or not. He had already lost the most important thing in his life.

The trial dragged on throughout the day. Smoothly guided by their attorney, both plaintiffs testified to damaged nerves, mental anguish, nightmares following the explosion of glass. The defense lawyer did his best to challenge them, but he knew it was hopeless. As he had feared, when Judge Barelli returned from the short recess he had called to ponder his decision, he made it quite clear that he considered Nicholas culpable for having set the stage for the accident.

"Were the real victim of this disregard for the safety precautions the litigant in this case, I would not hesitate to award her the full amount of the action," he said acerbically. "As it is, I'm cutting the award in half. I find for the plaintiffs in the amount of $250,000."

Casi drew a deep, shuddering breath and slipped out into the corridor the moment the verdict was announced. In her heart she felt certain that without her damaging testimony, the judgment against Nicholas would have been much less harsh. They had used her unscrupulously to get at him, prevailed on her to cut his throat for them. How bitter his feeling toward her must be now! The judge's words had erased any hope that they might ever be able to iron out their personal differences.

Three hours later, seated in a 747 winging its way across eastern Nevada, Casi was still reeling from the impact of that verdict. Numbly she tried to picture a quarter of a million dollars, attempted to imagine some way he could raise that enormous sum.

SINGLE-MINDEDLY Nicholas set about the monumental task confronting him. Losing Casi had shattered any chance for happiness he might ever have been able to achieve. He found her in his thoughts night and day. Every waking moment was tinged with regret. The hardest thing to bear was that he had brought it all on himself, from the very beginning. . . .

The one valued possession remaining to him was the land his grandfather had settled. This he was determined to save, by any means possible. If not for his own children, his and Casi's, then for Melina's.

In the first few weeks following the judgment he set about salvaging what he could with a cold-blooded intensity born out of desperation. He sold his car, his horse, the paintings off the wall and a collection of antique silver that Luisita had lovingly compiled over the last twenty years of her life. Aware of the reason for the offer, he swallowed his pride and accepted Vasco's bid for the twenty-acre parcel of level ground on the other side of the hill, where grapes were still grown. He surrendered every dollar in his savings account and beggared his checkbook to buy a little time.

During an all but sleepless ten-day period he completed the text to accompany his latest volume of photographs and couriered the parcel to his publisher with a plea for a sizable advance. The morning it arrived in the mail he opened a second letter. The envelope bore the logo of an eastern insurance company. Stapled to the enclosed form letter was a check for a staggering amount of money.

Eyeing it with mingled distress and relief, he realized that Casi must have arranged for him to be reimbursed for the amount he had spent settling her medical bills. Humbly he added his endorsement to the back of it. Combined with funds from the other sources he had tapped, the two checks allowed him to pay off four-fifths of the lawsuit's total.

But that last, still-gigantic portion of the debt threatened to be his undoing. Staring around at the bare walls of his home, Nicholas was forced to admit that he had nothing left except the land he had fought so hard to protect and his own skill with the camera. Arranging for a perilously short-term mortgage, he contacted his former news agency and volunteered to accept their most dangerous and thus most highly paid assignment.

Two days later, cameras slung over his shoulder, Nicholas was en route to Central America. His instructions were quite specific: he was to photograph every possible aspect of the volatile jungle warfare raging between Salvadorean revolutionaries and government factions.

One group was as ruthless as the other, and neither cared much for news photographers. Fatalistically, he faced up to the possiblility that his luck might run out this time. In that case it would be up to Melina and Dane to cope with the rest of the burden. He had already done the best he could.

11

"YOU'RE STILL dipping that shoulder, Doreen," Casi observed, attempting to keep the exasperation out of her voice. "Posture is a model's most valuable asset. When you come out of the turn your back should be straight. Like this." She demonstrated once more. "Try it again, please."

Watching the coltish seventeen-year-old revving up for another charge at the runway, she wondered dubiously whether the girl would ever make it in the world of high fashion. It was a tough, competitive business; thousands failed every year. Radiant beauty wasn't enough. A model needed to be sleek and effortless.

Tammy slipped inconspicuously into the room and stood behind her, observing their pupil's progress. "I can see a vast improvement since you started tutoring her," she said critically. "Do you still think she's wasting her tuition?"

Casi hesitated, not wanting to be the one to smash Doreen's dreams. "The ballet lessons have helped," she admitted. "At least she doesn't look like a diesel rig barreling down the turnpike nowadays. And she's a hard worker. Let's keep at it."

That was all anyone could do, she assured herself when the class ended five minutes later. Just keep at it. Plug away day after day and hope that things would improve. The advice sounded poignantly familiar. It was the same admonition she had been giving Casi Cavanaugh for the past two months.

Throughout the spring she had been struggling to put her own life back together again. Upon her return to New York she severed ties with her former agency and took an instructor's job at the modeling school Tammy and Grace had established. She found the meticulous work blessedly distracting. It used up eight hours a day, leaving her with only sixteen of the twenty-four to limp through in lonely solitude.

The three volumes that once held the place of honor on her coffee table were banished to the back shelf of a closet. She began work on a manuscript of her own: a how-to manual that she hoped might one day be used by aspiring models to help them get their careers off the ground. Six weeks of a night-school typing course had acquainted her with the mysteries of the keyboard. Each evening she spent several hours practicing, gradually increasing her dexterity and speed as she pecked away at the introductory pages of her textbook.

Unfortunately it wasn't as easy to eject Nicholas from her mind as it had been to shove his books out of sight. She knew it was self-destructive to allow memories of him to crowd everything else out of her thoughts, but all her efforts to forget him were futile. Irritated at this failure, Casi told herself to be logical. If she was going to think of him at all, it ought to be with indignation. He had shown an insulting lack of trust in her, betrayed her love with a false accusation.

Stern reminders such as these didn't have much effect, either. Her heart kept remembering the positive aspects of their bittersweet relationship. The patient way he had taught her to cope with the dark. Their bedtime chats over the airwaves. The incredible lengths he had gone to, trying to put himself in her place with a handkerchief tied over his eyes. The sheer, tingling joy of having him hold her, kiss her . . . make love to her.

Pain needled through her whenever she remembered that even then, during their happiest hours, she hadn't been fully content with the bliss he had offered. Instead she had fretted about losing her independence. She had actually complained to Melina about his overprotectiveness, really worried about allowing herself to be his pampered darling. In retrospect those fears seemed ridiculously petty. Now that it was too late, she would have given everything she possessed to be back in his arms, to have him spoiling her with slushy milkshakes and braiding sweet peas through her hair.

Those wonderful things had all vanished because of a few thoughtless words, spoken in haste, stubbornly resented at leisure.

The school was closing for the day. With another Wednesday under her belt, Casi picked up her purse and headed for the subway. The train was clogged with rush-hour commuters. Clinging to an overhead strap, she found herself sandwiched in the herd like a slab of cheese layered between slices of bread. Thanks to her height she had extra breathing room at least, and could easily peer over most people's shoulders. She did so now with the short, stocky man standing in front of her reading a news magazine.

Her eyes followed his down to the page, scanning the headlines as a way to relieve some of the jolting ride's tedium. "Fierce Jungle Warfare Erupts Anew in Central America," the banner screamed. Wasn't there any pleasant news in the world?

Casi started to glance away, then caught sight of the photographs illustrating the article. There was an eerie familiarity about them, as though she had seen similar shots before. Guerillas and terrorists were the same the world over, she thought, focusing harder on the inset illustrations. But not many cameramen would have...

"Oh, my God!" she gasped aloud, starting to tremble as a name printed beneath the top snapshot leapt off the page at her.

The man clutching the magazine darted an anxious look backward and up. "You ain't going to be carsick, are you, lady?" he muttered, eyeing her blanched face with suspicion.

"N-no, of course not," she stuttered in apology. "I just had a shock, that's all. Someone I know took those pictures, and I hadn't realized—" She tightened her grip on the strap to steady her wobbly limbs. "Would you show me the cover on that magazine, please? Or let me buy it from you?"

He edged away, but there was no place he could go in the tightly packed car. As if to humor her, he flipped back to the cover and held it up. It was the most current issue of *Time*. There ought to be some copies left on the newsstand.

"Thanks," she said, nodding weakly. "Sorry I troubled you."

He shouldered his way up the aisle at the next stop, still wearing the uneasy expression of a man who has had a close call getting involved in a stranger's problems. Casi didn't notice his departure. She had her eyes shut and was holding on in a daze now, willing herself to make it through the rest of this underground journey.

She hadn't been mistaken. Those were his photos, and it had been his name that riveted her attention. What was Nicholas doing in Central America, of all places? It was *dangerous* down there!

Relentlessly she canvased four newsstands before locating the magazine she sought. Unwilling to expose her transparent emotions to passersby, she forced herself to carry it back to her apartment before paging through to the lead article.

"Photographs by Nicholas Penheiro," the caption ran. She scanned the text, but the descriptions of death and torture in that snake-infested milieu increased her terror for him to the point where she found it difficult to catch her breath. He was there!

Blindly she reached for the telephone and started stabbing buttons before remembering that in California it was still the middle of the day. It took an extra ten minutes for her trembling fingers to run down the listings in her personal directory and find Melina's studio number. With a gigantic effort she took deep, calming breaths while someone at the other end went in search of the designer.

"Good to hear your voice," she said when the receiver was picked up. "How—how are you?"

"I'm fine. Waddling around in maternity clothes. Dane is well, too, but you sound all shook up," Melina said. "I'll bet you're holding a copy of *Time*."

"What is he doing down there?" Casi moaned.

"I thought you didn't care about Nicholas."

"You know I never said that! Melina—"

"He's on an assignment, Casi. It was the only way he could come up with the money to finish settling the lawsuit. He refused to let me sell my business, but he did put a short, balloon-payment mortgage on the ranch. If his luck holds, he hopes to get the debt cleared by September."

"'If his luck holds'!" For an hour Casi's heart had been thudding at an accelerated pace; now it felt as if it were about to hammer its way clear through her chest.

"Nicholas's words, not mine. He insisted this was something he had to take care of himself." Melina cleared her throat uncomfortably. "Nicholas specifically asked me not to say anything about this to you. I think he was afraid you might worry about him. For old times' sake. He told me that you'd agreed once not to hurt each other again, but that it had happened, anyway, and . . ."

"And what, Melina?"

"Well, he—he said that he didn't want there to be any more pain. On either side. That it was over, and—it was just over, that's all."

A single tear dredged a path down Casi's cheek and dropped unheeded to the desktop. "That's true," she said in a dead tone. "I knew when they handed me the subpoena that that would finish it."

"Oh, mercy, it wasn't only that. You were both so darned prickly— It's probably just as well, Casi. I love you both, but your temperaments did tend to clash a great deal." Melina sighed, then brightened. "However, that doesn't mean that you and I can't go on being good friends. By the way, I'm definitely holding you to your promise to be the baby's godmother."

"Sure," Casi said woodenly. "I wouldn't think of letting you down."

As soon as they hung up Casi took the magazine and pitched it into the trash. She didn't know what she was so upset about. For over two months now she'd been telling herself that their romance was ancient history. It shouldn't hurt this much simply to know that Nicholas felt the same way about it.

She remembered that pact they had made the first day he carried her down to the beach. They had promised not to hurt each other anymore. The road to hell was paved with good intentions, Casi thought miserably. That same day they had also decided to keep their relationship moving forward, not back.

Now it was really too late to go back. As he had said, it was over. Obviously she needed to start straightening out her emotions in a hurry, because she had no intention of standing shoulder to shoulder with Nicholas, holding Melina's baby and adding salty, bitter tears to the holy-water font!

In an all-out effort to mend her heart, Casi accepted dates with several of the bachelors who had been pursuing her before her life had been devastated by the California interlude. She allocated them one evening each and looked them over carefully, then said goodnight and goodbye on her doorstep. If anything, they seemed less interesting than ever.

But in resuming a sporadic social life she was at least trying to convince herself that Nicholas wasn't the only man in the world. Every time his name or face or voice rose to the surface of her consciousness she pushed it ruthlessly aside and made herself perform three difficult tasks.

The punishment helped. A little.

One Friday afternoon late in July, Grace stuck her head through the classroom door and beckoned Casi out into the hall.

"Doreen Robinson's father is here," she said. "He's willing to renew her tuition, but he'd like to meet you. I'll take over the group here while you go down to my office and have a talk with him."

This wasn't an unusual occurrence. At one time or another Casi had held conferences with the parents of most of the girls under her tutelage. Prepared for another such routine meeting, she entered Grace's office and closed the door.

The man who rose to greet her looked like someone who might have played defensive end for the Dallas Cowboys not too many years earlier. Thick, sandy hair drooped over his forehead, crinkling blue eyes beamed at her, and when he had completely unfolded himself from the chair she found herself looking up. Way up.

A grin broke over his freckled face as he held out his hand and took hers inside its welcoming clasp.

"Miss Cavanaugh, I've been wanting to meet you for the longest time. I'm certainly glad I finally got up the gumption to come over here," he said exuberantly. "My little girl keeps saying you're the prettiest lady in New York City. I can see now she has a bad habit of understating the facts. I've been back and forth across this country at least a dozen times, and I never—"

He broke off abruptly and let go of her hand. "'Scuse me, ma'am. I shouldn't have been so forward. My name's Wayne Robinson."

"Mr. Robinson, it's a pleasure." Casi smiled. Even without the obvious compliment she would have liked him on sight. "You have a sweet daughter. Sit down, please, and let's talk about the progress she's making with her courses."

He chuckled, a low, infectious rumble that made her lips tilt upward again. "No need to hash it over. I've seen the improvement with my own eyes. Back in Tulsa they'll never recognize that little ole tomboy who used to shinny up the oil derricks with me. No, sir! And it's all your doing!"

"Thank you. I'm glad you're so pleased." Perplexed, Casi watched him fiddling with the brim of his Stetson. "Did you have any questions I could answer for you?"

"Yes, ma'am." It seemed impossible that anyone so huge could look so bashful. "I was wondering whether you'd do me the honor of being my dinner partner to-night."

"I'm sorry, Mr. Robinson," Casi said politely but firmly. "I never go out with married men."

All the colors of a sunset in the West flared across his face.

"Miss Cavanaugh, I have the highest respect for those kinds of ideals. I should have mentioned right off that I'm a widower. Doreen's mamma has been with the angels eleven years now." He shifted uncomfortably to the other boot. Up until just recently I've been busy bringing in gushers and raising my daughter."

"Oh, I see. In that case, I'd like very much to go. On one condition."

"Anything you say, ma'am."

"That you stop using 'ma'am' and start calling me 'Casi'!"

WAYNE ROBINSON certainly went all out, Casi thought, tipping the delivery boy who had just presented her with another huge box filled with American Beauty roses. She felt almost guilty snipping off a portion of their long stems to fit them into her tallest vase.

Standing back to survey the arrangement, admiring the velvety texture of the scarlet buds, contrasted with the lacy green ferns and delicate white clusters of baby's breath, she decided she had never seen anything quite so heavenly.

An unwelcome thought tiptoed into her mind. Nicholas had sent her roses, too. Every day while she was in the hospital. His flowers had probably been just as lovely as these. The only trouble was, she hadn't been able to see them. All she could do then was inhale their fragrance.

She bent toward the tall crystal urn, taking a deep breath of the perfumed scent. If she closed her eyes she could almost imagine . . .

Annoyed at herself, she opened her eyes to their widest and hurried into the bedroom to finish dressing. In the six weeks she had been dating Wayne she had learned that punctuality was one of his many virtues. Exactly eighteen minutes from now he was going to present himself at the door. When he did, she wanted him to find her looking her best. A man as gallantly attentive as Doreen's father deserved to squire around "the prettiest lady in New York City." It was challenging trying to live up to Doreen's billing.

Casi sprayed on a mist of Arpège and slithered into a floor-length black taffeta sheath. The dress was an exquisitely feminine concoction, one of the few things she'd purchased for herself in a long time, with a deeply scalloped neckline and arm-molding sleeves that tapered to a deep V at her wrists. The lush ebony hue of the rustling fabric contrasted dramatically with the translucent whiteness of her shoulders and brought out the richness of her natural coloring.

Tonight her long auburn hair was piled on top of her head except for one tightly curled ringlet left to dangle seductively along each side of her oval face. Fastening the clasp of a shimmering gold necklace set with small, square-cut emeralds exactly matching the color of her eyes, she stepped back for a final appraisal. Not bad at all, she thought in satisfaction. Wayne was going to be pleased.

She was just slipping on a pair of evening slippers, when the phone rang. A voice from out of the past responded to her hello.

"Say congratulations to the new father," Dane boomed. "Melina just presented me with a beautiful baby boy!"

"How fantastic!" Casi squealed. "Congratulations to both of you. And to the baby, too, for having such great parents. Is Melina okay?"

"Sitting up and ordering the nurses around already." Dane laughed. "She says to tell you the christening has been set for Saturday after next. The eighteenth. We're calling the baby Eric, after my Dad."

"Super name. Everything sounds wonderful. Has—" Casi heard the doorbell chime and suppressed the question she had been about to ask. "Never mind. I'll call and get the rest of the details in a few days. Get back to Melina now. Give her a kiss for me."

She hung up and nearly danced to the door, overjoyed by the good news. As soon as she swung it open, Wayne reacted to her appearance with a dazed look.

"My goodness, Casi, you are one gorgeous female!" he said with a whistle, stepping into the room and pulling the door shut behind him. "Honey, I hope you don't mind my messing up your war paint, but I just can't keep my hands to myself with you looking that fabulous."

He swept her into a masterful embrace, kissing her with a feverish passion that warned Casi he would probably go all out when it came to making love, too. She stood on tiptoe to meet his lips, responding with as much ardor as she could muster on the spur of the moment. Wayne was a thoroughly nice man, she told herself. He would make a marvelous husband. And after bringing up Doreen by himself, he'd already proved what a terrific father he could be. He was handsome and rich and eight inches taller than she. Absolutely perfect.

"Hey," she said softly, pulling back. "We're going to miss the curtain."

"That Broadway show went clean out of my mind." Wayne dropped his arms and reached for his handkerchief. "Come to think of it, the taxi driver is still waiting downstairs. Guess we'd better be on our way."

The musical comedy fully deserved its rave reviews, and the evening of dinner and dancing at an exclusive supper club that followed was thoroughly enjoyable.

"Every man in this room wishes he could trade places with me right now," Wayne declared, twirling her around in time to the music. "I surely would be proud to show you off to Tulsa."

Forewarned by that clue, Casi had a little time to prepare herself for what she knew would be coming when they got back to her apartment. Wayne was going to propose. He had planned this gala night especially, to make it memorable in every way.

She'd be proud to be his wife. They'd have a wonderful life together. No fights, no arguments. As compatible as they were, they couldn't miss.

En route home in the cab, she told him about the phone call from California. "It's their first baby, and of course the whole family is all excited. I'll be flying to San Francisco for the christening on the eighteenth of this month."

"That's two weeks from today." Wayne took her key and unlocked the door, ushering her inside. Gently he tugged her down on the couch beside him. "The timing could be mighty convenient if you wanted it to be."

Casi's wide emerald eyes took in the sincerity on his face, the endearing splatter of freckles across his nose. She had never met a man she liked better. "I'm not sure what you mean, Wayne."

"I was thinking that maybe you could take me along with you. After the christening we'd keep on going. We could visit Tahiti and Australia and China, if you like the idea. Make it a round-the-world honeymoon."

His crinkly blue eyes gazed deeply into hers. "Beautiful lady, I'm asking you to be my wife. I love you. Doreen loves you, too. Matter of fact, she's the one who lassoed me out here to meet you. Said she had finally found the right woman to be her new mamma."

"What a lovely compliment," Casi whispered. He was so right for her, she thought. A really wonderful man.

"Would you like a little time to think about it before you give me your answer?"

No woman in her right mind would refuse him. Casi Robinson. Casi and Wayne. Even their names sounded good together.

She held out her hand and urged him up off the couch, then walked with him across the room, where she flipped on the stereo to a romantic music station.

"Would you do something for me?"

"I'll lay the world at your feet, Casi. You just tell me what you want."

"Dance with me. And talk to me at the same time." She looked up at him beseechingly. "It's kind of important, Wayne. A few months ago I made myself a promise, and I'd—I'd like to follow through on it."

Wayne cuddled her head against his shoulder as their feet moved and their bodies began to sway to the tempo.

"Casi, love, if you want to keep on teaching at that modeling school it's okay with me. Or I'll buy you one of your own." His lips brushed her hair. "I know women value their careers nowadays same as men. We'll settle out on Long Island, maybe. Build us a big, fancy mansion. Fill it up with kids, if you're willing. Do you like kids?"

"I love kids," Casi murmured, squeezing her eyes shut, listening with all her heart. He was offering her love, security, independence, a family. He could give her everything. Everything except those icy shivers up and down her spine that the mere thought of Nicholas could produce.

"Then we'll have lots. Four or five. You call the shots. We'll get us a nanny to give you a hand with the diapers and what not. Leave you with plenty of free time to keep on looking beautiful, the way you do tonight."

Casi smoothed her fingers across his broad, square shoulders, ordering her pulse to race. He was all muscle. Not an ounce of flab. Her hands should love touching those hard, masculine sinews.

She inhaled deeply, savoring his particular scent. Clean. Manly. Why didn't it stir her sentiments? She considered biting at the buttons of ruffled white shirt to catch a taste of him, but abandoned that last-ditch attempt. It wasn't any use. So long as she kept her eyes open she could tell herself that Wayne was the perfect man for her. The minute she closed them and started making use of her other senses, the four Nicholas had aroused to the point of frenzy, she knew that she had been lying to herself.

"We'll take the young'uns out to the ranch near Tulsa every summer, and—"

"Oh, stop, please!" Casi moaned. Every time she listened, every time they tried to make love, she would be unfaithful to him in her thoughts. For her their marriage would forever be a second-best kind. He would know. She could never hide it from him. And he deserved better.

The music went on uninterrupted, but Wayne had come to a standstill. "The answer's no, isn't it, Casi?" he asked sadly.

She drew back her head, tormented tears brimming in her emerald eyes. "Dear Wayne, I like you so very much. I wish—"

"You wish you loved me, but there's somebody else. I've known it all along. Every once in a while your face takes on that faraway look, as if maybe you've got a secret worry buried deep inside you. I just kept hoping I was mistaken."

That wretched cellophane expression of hers, giving everything away!

"You weren't mistaken," she said, confirming his worst fears. "We called it quits six months ago. We hurt each other pretty badly, and he went off to do something dangerous. I do worry—constantly." She gulped down devastating waves of emotion. "He doesn't love me anymore, but... There isn't anything I can do about it, Wayne. I've tried and tried...."

He kissed her tenderly one last time. "Chin up, beautiful lady. If the day ever comes when you change your mind, you just give me a whistle out in Tulsa, hear?"

"I hear." Casi tilted her jaw a fraction of an inch. "I hear. It's just my stubborn heart that refuses to listen."

IT SEEMED STRANGE to be driving over the bridge, actually seeing those amber girders, the sparkling waters of the bay far below, Marin's golden hills ahead of her. Last February the winter rains had turned the hills green, she remembered. After that her crossings had been made in darkness.

Now, at summer's end, the long grasses tufting the hillsides had mellowed, seared to a brittleness. The desiccated blades rippled in the midday breeze, beckoning her on toward the small town church where the baptismal ceremony was to be held.

She had flown in the previous night and slept over at an airport hotel. This morning she had rented the car, an easy-to-handle Ford Escort. Zipping past the unmanned tollgate, Casi droned through the tunnel and shortly afterward turned left, in accordance with Dane's instructions.

When she had phoned him a week ago, the baby had been squawling in the background. It had been all she could do to make sense of the directions he was giving her, nail down the time she was supposed to arrive. There had been no opportunity to fit in that one extra query that was uppermost in her mind.

Had Nicholas come home? Would he be there today? Or would a proxy stand in for him as godfather? She could only wonder. She hoped he was safe and well. But really, Casi told herself sensibly, it would be better if she didn't have to stand next to him, repeating the vows they would make for their infant charge. That would be too reminiscent of another set of vows, which they had never gotten around to exchanging.

And never would. "It's over," he had told Melina. No more pain on either side. He couldn't possibly know the anguish that statement had caused her in the past few months, couldn't possibly realize that for her there would never be anyone else. For her it would never be over.

Casi's pulse was a relentless jackhammer in her wrist. The insistent throb of excitement battered at her carefully erected defenses. She wanted him to be present. Oh, so much! She ached to see him, to fill her eyes with him. Just this once.

Searching for landmarks, she caught sight of the steeple, and pulled into the nearly empty parking lot. Several cars were clustered in front of the church's side door. She pointed the Escort in the same direction and let it roll to a stop. Half an hour early.

Casi tilted the rearview mirror to catch a reflection of her face. The white scars had faded almost to invisibility. She wore a touch of lip gloss, a delicate wisp of mascara to darken her too-fair lashes. Probably nobody would recognize her. For the camera she had always worn tons of makeup, at the sea ranch none at all. Now, like the role she would fulfill today, neither family member nor stranger, she was somewhere in between those two extremes.

She stepped out of the car, smoothing down the skirt of her white, sheer wool dress with its boat back and cap sleeves, and reached across the seat for the green blazer to slip on over it. Her high-heeled pumps had been dyed to match.

Tossing her free-flowing hair back over the jacket's starchy collar, she picked up her handbag and turned toward the church.

Her foot had barely crossed into the shaded vestibule, when she saw him. She caught her breath, feeling her heart lurch. In profile he looked much too lean in the gray suit. A blue silk tie was knotted underneath his white collar. His face was even browner than she had remembered it from long ago, before her dark time, when exterior appearances had temporarily ceased to matter.

Standing a little apart from Dane and Melina, arms folded across his chest, his expression was solemn. She wondered if he ever smiled, or if those laugh lines had been an illusion her fingers had conjured up so long ago. Searching the shadows of his face, she watched as a stray beam pierced the stained-glass window, illuminating his forehead and highlighting the blue-black of his crisp wavy hair.

Casi took a long, deep breath to combat her sudden dizziness. Feeling an urgent need for oxygen she repeated the action. Then, reminding herself of the plan she had formulated to shield herself from further agony, she forced her quaking legs to move forward.

She had taken only two more steps before he turned, as if sensing her presence, and trapped her in the intensity of his dark gaze.

Even if she had wanted to it was too late to look away now. Sure that the thudding of her heart would have been outwardly visible if not for her loose jacket, Casi walked toward him. Neither of them changed expression. This wasn't so hard, she reassured herself. Seeing him now she could remember the old Nicholas, the one she hadn't liked.

Melina raised her head and gave a cry of welcome. "Casi, come and meet your godson! This is Eric!"

Nothing else could have dragged her eyes away from Nicholas, made her detour from her and Nicholas's collision course. There was no resisting that baby. He was infinitely precious. Casi held out her arms, clasping the drowsy infant to her breast. Her lips parted wonderingly as she surveyed his tiny, perfect features. A fuzz of raven hair drifted over Eric's head, but the cheekbones were unmistakably Scandinavian.

"He's the best of both of you!" she exclaimed in delight.

Behind her, Nicholas swung his head back to the empty doorway and tightened the grip he had taken on himself. He should have stayed in the jungle for another week, he thought hopelessly. The bullets, snakes and quicksand he had frequently encountered in that tropical hell seemed mere trifles compared with the sensation of despair that hit him when she'd walked past without stopping.

The anteroom filled rapidly as family and friends gathered to witness the ceremony. A whole countyful of people must be present, Casi decided. She wondered how many of them she would know if they spoke. That chubby, older couple across the way could easily be Soledad and Vasco. And two or three of the younger women were absolutely gorgeous—which of them was Olivia?

Like the Red Sea parting, the group made way for Father Albrecht. "Godparents, please come forward," he instructed, moving toward the cherub-bedecked font. "Godmother is already holding the baby? Excellent. Godfather, stand next to her. Now parents . . ."

Massive shoulders moved alongside Casi's. Unable to restrain the impulse, she turned her head to look at him. The three-inch heels plus her own six feet of height brought her eyes almost even with his.

"You're so thin," she murmured. "Didn't those people down there feed you?"

"When they could. It's a land of terrible poverty." Emerald and black, their eyes locked. "Did my sister tell you?"

Casi shook her head. "Someone in the subway was reading a newsmagazine. Those on-the-spot photos were unmistakably yours. I nearly passed out when I saw your name on the credit line." Her eyes fluttered shut, trying to block out that terrible memory.

"You're looking terrific. I guess the milkshakes must have helped a little."

Nicholas saw her yank her eyes open quickly as he started to speak. Their depths shimmered mistily. She hadn't wanted him to know she'd been worried, he supposed. Merely for old times' sake, of course. But why not keep them closed, so he wouldn't notice the tender-hearted concern?

"Casi—"

"We're ready to begin," the priest intoned.

The christening rite, with its roots in the ancient tradition of John the Baptist fulfilling his destiny at the Sea of Galilee, commenced. Knowing the responses expected of them, the godparents turned their minds to the service.

Melina and Dane supplied the baby's name, answering in unison the questions asked of them. Eric waved a tiny fist when his chest was annointed with oil and kicked at the blanket while his godparents promised to make sure he was raised in the Catholic faith should anything happen to his parents before he was fully grown.

Speaking for the baby, Casi and Nicholas responded to the vows, their "I do's" promising to reject Satan, all his works and all his empty promises.

Eric let out a thin, wailing cry when the trickles of water were poured ritualistically over his head. Casi clutched him more tightly, steadying the wiggling body. Then the ceremony was over. In relief she turned away from the font and held out the child to his mother.

"Everybody's invited to the champagne party at our house," Melina bubbled to the group at large. She turned back to Casi, offering her a personal invitation. "Leave your car here and ride with us. It's been far too long since we've seen you, and we have months' worth of conversation to catch up on."

Her attendance at the party was expected, Casi realized. It would be a slap in her friends' faces if she tried to pull out now. Undoubtedly they would want to take pictures for Eric's baby book.

The Jorgensens piled into the front seat of Dane's sedan. Holding the back door for Casi, Nicholas watched for a moment as her long, tapering fingers searched for the seat belt. She kept her eyes on her lap while she dragged the canvas strap across her middle and shoved the two ends together. Swallowing hard, repelling memories of another time he had seen her perform that particular task, he strode around back to climb in the other side.

Melina kept up a constant stream of chatter as the car snaked along the curving road to the beach. It was an understandably exciting day for her, and she leap-frogged from one subject to another with such rapidity that no one else had a chance to say anything.

In a few minutes the wafting sea breeze became much more noticeable. It brought with it tinges of salt, seaweed, fish—and memories of feet scrunching through the sand, the play of her fingers across the ridgy whorls of an abalone. Casi's lids drooped as she inhaled nostalgically. They had walked along talking, promising....

She snapped open her eyes abruptly; thoughts such as those had the power to destroy her! She fastened her attention on the wild, open landscape where no disturbing reminders could be found.

A puzzled frown furrowed Nicholas's brow. Twice now Casi had done that—closed her eyes, then opened them immediately. He didn't remember that mannerism from before, and he had spent days peering at her through his camera lens. An aftereffect of her surgery. No, this was something deliberate. Strange....

The car swung onto a side road. Casi stayed alert for a bark as ruts clamped the wheels. But none came. Then, unable to keep her head from swinging to the right, she found herself staring at a long, low house with a fringe of lush greenery draping across its arches. The red tile roof glistened in the afternoon sun, casting shadows across the veranda.

She knew exactly how it smelled, that house. The yeasty odor of baking bread from the kitchen, the fragrance of sweet peas wafting through the open patio door.

And she knew how it felt. The grooved wood paneling bumping her fingers as they trailed across it. The well-worn arms of the old rocking chair, polished to a glassy smoothness by generations of hands rubbing along its surface. That loose button on one end of the comfortable old couch. The bed that . . .

Jaw tightening, she turned her head back toward the whitecapped Pacific and caught him watching her. Mind reading? She hoped not.

Theirs was the first car in the cavalcade. Cradling the baby, Melina stepped out as soon as Dane held the door for her. The two of them hastened ahead to throw open the house for their guests.

In an unhurried manner Nicholas unfolded his long body. By the time he had gathered up the presents that had been transferred from Casi's rental car to the sedan's trunk and come around to courteously open the door on her side, the couple was already out of sight.

Casi slid out, fastening her eyes on the ground. "Gravel path, forty feet. Then three low steps," she mused half-aloud, echoing a description that took her back in time. She raised her head to meet Nicholas's eyes. "Did I ever thank you for helping me to find my way around blindfolded? If not—"

A racy sports car angled in to the side of the road and stopped. A stunning young woman with black curly hair and a beaming expression swung gracefully out and called a greeting.

"Casi! Great to see you again!"

This was a park ranger? She belonged on the cover of *Vogue!* "You've got to be Olivia," Casi said. "I'm so glad—"

Olivia stretched out both arms in friendly welcome. There wasn't a cloud in the sky to block out the sunlight, not so much as a shadow to prevent the dazzling rays of the sun from striking all fifty-eight facets of the diamond solitaire on the girl's left hand.

Casi saw the ring flash by as Olivia wrapped her arms around her. There was nothing she could do except respond like a well-mannered guest . . . the godmother, on deck for this one occasion only.

She hugged Olivia in return, but for her all the brightness had suddenly drained out of the day.

12

RIGID WITH SHOCK, Casi politely disentangled herself from the girl's enthusiastic hug and avoided Nicholas's eyes as the three of them mounted the steps and went inside. Behind them other car doors slammed loudly. Crowds of people carrying blue-bowed baby gifts began streaming up the path at their heels. Unconscious of the tension her arrival had caused, Olivia continued to chat in a friendly, eager manner, babbling away about the litter of puppies they had taken Casi to "see" that last afternoon.

Fortunately no response seemed to be necessary. Casi crossed the tile and proceeded numbly toward the kitchen, thinking how lucky it was she had learned to find her way around this house with a mask over her eyes. Right now she was moving like a windup toy, a mechanical robot.

"What can I do to help?" she asked Melina.

With the baby clasped over her shoulder, Melina had already started pulling covered trays of food from the refrigerator and was ferrying them over to the table.

"Let's get the goodies laid out so people can serve themselves when they're ready to eat." The hostess looked up in distraction. "Nicholas, would you give Dane a hand pouring the champagne? Here, Olivia, please take these glasses into the living room."

Casi moved automatically through the necessary tasks, pulling plastic wrap away from earlier prepared piles of finger sandwiches, arranging dishes of hors d'oeuvres buffet-style in a circle around the lavishly decorated cake that formed the centerpiece, laying silverware and napkins out on the sideboard.

It was a beautiful engagement ring, she thought. No wonder Olivia looked so happy. No wonder Nicholas hadn't said a word to her since they'd left the church. He was probably trying to think of a tactful way to invite her to the wedding.

The plump little lady she had glimpsed at the ceremony did indeed turn out to be Soledad. She, too, greeted Casi like a long-lost friend. Then, within thirty seconds of entering the kitchen, she had an apron on and was flapping it at her and Melina.

"I'll take care of the hot dishes. You two get out there with the guests and enjoy the celebration. Shoo!"

Dane shoved a glass of champagne into her hand as soon as she entered the living room. "What do you think of our little boy?" he asked, beaming euphorically. "Tell me the truth. Isn't he the best-looking baby you've ever seen?"

Touched by his obvious pride, Casi worked up an enthusiastic smile for his benefit. "An absolute prize-winner! You and Melina produced a real treasure, Dane."

"As Eric's uncle, I second the opinion." Nicholas moved forward to take a glass off the tray. He lifted it in a salute and raised his voice to carry across the assembled throng, getting their attention in order to propose a toast to the new parents.

"May the Jorgensens always be as happy as they are today. And may there be many little brothers and sisters for Eric to play with in the future!"

Bringing her glass to her lips, Casi sipped to wish them well. When she set it back on the tray, her fingers accidentally brushed Nicholas's. With an inward gasp she pulled her hand back in a hurry. But his all-too-close presence was impossible to ignore. Feeling like a magnet next to a mass of steel, she found her head lifting, turning.

The expression in his glittering black eyes was unfathomable. To keep her fingers from trembling, she locked them once more around the stem of the goblet. Maybe it was the bubbles fizzing that distorted her perceptions, but it seemed to her that the deep breath he took was in preparation for something he wanted to say.

Time to break the bad news, perhaps. Stoically she stood her ground, giving him a chance to get it off his chest.

Melina reached between them to replace her empty glass. "You'd better get those pictures taken, Dane, before we put the baby down for his nap," she said. "No, honey, not in here. Go out back where you won't need to use the flash cubes."

Once again Casi found herself with her godson cooing in her arms, as Dane urged her and Nicholas out into the yard. He removed the flash attachment from his camera and fussily posed the threesome in a sunny spot at the edge of the fuchsia-bordered patio where no shadows could intrude to spoil the shots.

"Move in closer to them, Nicholas. You're too far apart," Dane complained from beyond the barbecue.

"We've been too far apart for a long time," Nicholas murmured in a voice just loud enough for her ears alone to catch. His hard, strong body pressed her side as he took one of Eric's dimpled hands in his own large fist.

Casi flinched in anguish when she felt his other arm slide around her for the camera's benefit. She couldn't endure much more of this torture. It felt as if this day would never end. With a gigantic effort she composed her stiff face into a smile. The shutter clicked.

"I guess congratulations are in order," she said, tilting her chin, edging her voice with frosty politeness.

"Hold it. I want to get a few more shots from different angles," Dane called.

"What for?" Nicholas asked her distantly. "Because I came home in one piece?"

Dane's tone sounded exasperated. "Quit wiggling, dammit! I'm not a professional photographer, just a nervous new father. Can't you two hold still and smile? The baby's the only one who looks happy."

"Think of sharks," Nicholas hissed. "He'll get a great smile out of you that way."

"You don't need to rub it in just because I'm a lousy actress!"

Inching her shoulder away from his, Casi rearranged her expression into a lopsided grin. The result was a long way from being a happy-occasion beam, but it was the best she could manage.

"Wouldn't you know? I'm out of film," Dane grumbled. "You guys stay right there while I go reload the camera."

"All right," Casi groaned in resignation.

"The hell with that," Nicholas said, reversing her decision. "Eric is getting a sunburn and I want to talk to his godmother. Why don't you take him inside, Dane? We'll get all the pictures you want later on."

Casi's first inclination was to dart away as soon as the baby was removed from her arms. An iron grip on her shoulder pinned her to the spot. It wasn't until the screen door had banged behind his brother-in-law that Nicholas removed his hand and instantly grabbed hers with it, pulling her toward the side gate.

"What do you think you're doing?" she protested.

"I'm going to have a private conversation with you if I have to haul you all the way to the top of Mount Tamalpais to do it," he growled, dragging her along.

Casi dug in her heels. "I doubt that your fiancée would approve!"

"Who cares what—"

Nicholas came to such an abrupt halt that she plowed into him. "Is that what those snide congratulations were all about? Olivia's engagement ring?"

"Certainly. Don't you know anything about etiquette?" she snapped, backing away. "People are supposed to congratulate the man and tell the bride-to-be they hope she'll be very happy. You tell her for me. I hope she'll be very happy with you."

"Now who's jumping to conclusions?"

She tried to snatch her hand away, but the pressure of his fingers only increased.

"Answer me, Casi! Tell me you actually believed I could marry somebody else after what happened between us!"

All the starch went out of her as the impact of that fierce question reverberated through her consciousness. She could feel her shoulders starting to shake, her chin beginning to wobble.

"I did think that, yes," she whispered. "If I was wrong, I apologize."

"You were wrong," Nicholas said flatly, giving her a none-too-gentle push through the gate and latching it behind them. "The same way I was wrong when I stupidly believed that you intended to sue me."

The cloyingly sweet odor of alternating red and white oleander bushes near the front walk assaulted her nostrils as she was steered past them. The landscaping was new since she'd been here last, Casi thought inconsequentially. The slick soles of her new shoes skidded on a damp clump of grass, nearly landing her in a bottle-brush plant.

Nicholas didn't give her the chance to come up with a suitable reply. "Olivia's fiancé is a twenty-three-year-old kid in the park service named Josh MacKenzie," he growled, and she could see a tense muscle bulging in his jaw. "I don't know about the Cavanaughs, but people in my family only get one chance at a grand passion. We don't treat it lightly!"

"Are you insinuating that I take things lightly?" Casi dragged her feet in a braking action to slow him down. "Listen, I was invited here for a party, and—"

There was no opportunity to finish the sentence. Nicholas swung around, lifted her into the air as easily as if she had been his infant nephew and kept right on heading down the road.

"That party's going to last all day," he said grimly. "You can go back when we've had this out once and for all. Every time I've started to speak to you today, someone else has beaten me to the punch. I intend to see that we're not interrupted again!"

A feeling of total helplessness pervaded Casi's numbed senses. Time after time he had carried her along this route in the past, but on those earlier occasions his touch had been affectionate. Gentle. Protective. There was certainly no resemblance between the way he had held her then and the viselike grip he was using now. In those days he had stopped frequently to kiss her, whisper words of love to her. Now his silent lips were a hard, implacable line, and it was doubtful whether even a barbed-wire fence would have slowed him down.

Not wanting to give him the satisfaction of struggling, Casi stared out into space and clasped her hands in front of her, refusing to let them so much as brush against his clothing. It was bad enough having her arm and shoulder rub across his chest with every stride he took, punishment enough to have his iron fingers clamped around her knees, mashing them into his jacket. She could make it easier for him, of course, by putting her arm around his neck, leaning her head against his shoulder, but she wasn't about to cooperate in her own abduction. He was lucky she was too dignified to kick and scream!

"I can't imagine why you're going to all this trouble," she said coldly, keeping her eyes pinned on the surging ocean far below the cliff. "It doesn't seem to me that we have anything to talk about. You distinctly told your sister that it was all over between us."

"Maybe it is. We'll see."

He marched onto the veranda of his house, lugged her through the door and snapped the lock behind them.

Suddenly he seemed to run out of steam. With a heavy sigh, he set her down on her feet and shoved his hands into his pockets.

"Here's your chance to see my face on a Wanted poster." He tossed the words in her direction like a challenge. "You could probably have me run in for kidnapping."

All at once Casi's pent-up emotions jerked loose of their constraints. "If you think I'm ever going into court to testify against you again—" She swiveled her head away from him, mashing her hands against her face in a fruitless attempt to shove the tears back inside her eyelids.

Nicholas's sudden intake of breath sounded pained, as though it hurt him to breathe. "Don't do that. Please." Awkwardly he reached out a tentative hand to smooth her hair.

"Well, how would you have felt if they'd kept hammering away at you, making you say things that hurt other people?"

"It would have torn my heart out. Casi, I knew you weren't up there on that witness stand because you wanted to be. As it was, you came pretty close to perjury, trying to get them to go easy on me." He fastened his eyes on the floor to hide the anguish in them. "What hurt the worst that day was that you wouldn't even look in my direction."

"Do you know what would have happened if I had? That lawyer would have read my thoughts as if they were printed on cue cards!" Casi gave a muffled wail. "I couldn't let him suspect—"

"That you were more than just the image in my lens?" Taking both her hands in his, Nicholas lowered them, then bent forward and gently smoothed the tears away from her cheeks with his fingertips. "Are we going to stand out here in the hall all day, or would you rather sit down somewhere and talk this out?"

"That's why you kidnapped me, isn't it?"

Nicholas suppressed a snarl of despair. He dragged his hands away from her face, clenching them into fists. Where she was concerned, he had always been a blundering fool. All week long he had been telling himself he had one chance, one last chance, to try to make amends. Now, as usual, he had botched it.

He swallowed, forcing evenness into his tone. "I apologize for the caveman tactics. If you want to leave, I'll carry you back up the hill myself." He turned toward the door, then paused with his hand on the dead bolt and fastened his eyes on her face. "It was just so damned frustrating, not being able to get a word in edgeways! I figured this was our only chance to straighten things out."

Straighten things out? Dear God, if only she thought there were a prayer of that! But where could they start? What could she say that wouldn't resurrect some ghastly pain?

With Nicholas there was no subject that didn't hurt. And long ago she had finished playing games with the language. Casi raised her head and met his eyes, getting the worst topic out of the way first. "You really don't hold my testimony for the prosecution against me?"

A rueful smile touched his lips. "You did a better job than the defense attorney. Without you they'd have collected the whole half a million." He gestured around at the empty walls, whose lighter patches of paint gave mute testimony to the pictures that had once hung there. "Maybe I'd better tell you right now that I'm flat broke, but out of debt."

He couldn't possibly think money had anything to do with her feelings, Casi thought. To share that old happiness she'd live in a boxcar with him. In a tent on the beach!

"I'm proud of you, Nicholas. You did a terrific job of paying off those greedy wolves."

With anyone else, he might have been able to brush the statement aside as mere tact. But Casi didn't know how to lie. She meant it. The fact that he didn't have a nickel right now didn't matter to her a bit. Something else still rankled, though. The fact that once he hadn't been able to take her on faith.

He gazed at her through tormented eyes. "Casi, there hasn't been one minute of the past six months that I haven't regretted what I said to you that day out on the road. It was the meanest, most unforgivable—"

"No," Casi protested. "I should have—"

They both stopped, choking down emotion.

"Will you let me say I'm sorry?" Nicholas asked at last.

Blinking rapidly, Casi nodded. "How about me? We're both terrible conclusion jumpers. I'm sorry, too. Sorry for . . . everything."

She reached over and removed his hand from the dead bolt, leaving it locked. The touch of his skin was heartbreakingly familiar, warm and wonderful in every way. Yet though her fingers tingled reminiscently just from that light contact, it seemed so peculiar to be standing there face-to-face with the man she loved and actually seeing him. This wasn't the way she remembered it being; this wasn't the same. . . .

Casi's eyelids fluttered down. Time lapsed, and she was back, back where she wanted to be. She increased the pressure on his hand, starting to pull him closer so her arms could fasten lovingly around his neck. The gesture was a reflex born out of longing.

Suddenly it dawned on her what had almost happened. Once things were over you couldn't go back! She yanked her eyes open again and, catching sight of his startled face, took a step away from him.

"*That's* what you've been doing!" Nicholas whispered intensely. He wrapped his arms around her shoulders, drawing her nearer inch by inch. "I finally figured it out!"

"Wha-what are you talking about?"

"You know what I'm talking about, Casi. As long as you kept your eyes open I was practically a stranger. Not somebody who meant anything in particular, right? But every now and then you wanted so badly to close them and go back to the beautiful way it was for us once. . . . That's it, isn't it, Casi?"

Trapped, knowing how useless it was to try to lie to him, she bobbed her head. "It only happened a couple of times."

"Three," Nicholas insisted. "You were fighting it all the way, but I saw you do it three times."

He had her right up against his chest now. He held her still for a long minute, then slid his hands along her arms, urging them to curl up around his neck.

"Allow me to introduce myself," he breathed. "Hold on tight, sweetheart, and keep your eyes open."

He bent his head, covering her lips with his. His kiss, that hot, passionate means of communication that she had once insisted should be copyrighted, jolted her once and for all into realizing that the real Nicholas Penheiro stood here in her arms. There could only be one of him, this unique, wonderful man. Stern photographer merged subtly, firmly, into the friend, companion, teacher, lover whom her ears and fingers and nose and mouth had so adored.

It was like the Fourth of July instead of just past Labor Day. Roman candles exploded; pinwheels spiraled around in Casi's head. She ran her fingers across his broad shoulders, exulting in the touch of him. This was Nicholas, gloriously real. Against hers, his mouth was achingly familiar. With every movement of lips and tongue it was satisfying a half year's thirst and simultaneously wreaking new havoc throughout her quivering body.

She didn't dare close her eyes. He was watching her. Obediently Casi flared them wide and enjoyed little peeks of him, kaleidoscopic glimpses of nose and ear, cheek and eyebrow. Nicholas's hands had crept up underneath her hair. With slow, sensual movements he was caressing her nape, petting the little hollow there with a vibrating stroke that brought a shivery recollection of their hands-on encounter zinging into her mind.

It was glorious to be in his arms again. How she had ever survived the torment of separation was beyond her. Casi's fingers sought the sides of his face, ruffling the arc of his sideburns. A moan escaped her lips at the erotic stimulation the sharp little hairs keyed in her imagination.

Still holding her in a loving embrace, Nicholas lifted his mouth away from hers. "That's a much better way to get acquainted than with a handshake, wouldn't you say?"

Casi filled her eyes with the sight of him, trying to quiet the fluttering sensations deep inside her. It took more than a minute for her breathing to quiet down to the point where she could move her lips again, form coherent words into a vitally important question.

"Nicholas, I have to know. Did you mean it—what you told Melina?"

"That's almost as insulting as thinking I'd marry Olivia—marry anyone, love anyone, except you. Casi, I didn't mean it. I was whistling in the dark, trying to protect my stupid ego from my sister's sympathy."

Holding him tight, she shuddered in relief.

"Casi, I love you so much it's killing me." Nicholas folded her to his chest again, kissing her ear, her eyebrow, dragging his lips along the curve of her cheek. "I never quit loving you, darling, not for one second of the time we were apart. Every day it got worse. No matter where I was, what I was doing—"

He brought his mouth down on hers with a hungry, crushing force that was more convincing than any words could have been. Defenses scuttled, no longer needed or wanted, Casi closed her eyes and turned her emotions loose at last, pressing her lips against his with a ferocity that threatened bruises. Her hands wiggled in underneath his suit jacket, questing fingers massaging the warm, strong division of his back.

When at long last Nicholas came up for air, his black eyes were slumberous with desire. "It's been terrible without you." He shuddered. "I was convinced I had lost you forever."

He shook his head and touched her cheek as though she were made of fragile porcelain. "I've found my grand passion, Casi. You're the only woman I'll ever love. For me it's not going to be over until the day I die."

Casi's loving emerald eyes beamed at him. Her tremulous laugh betrayed how deeply his words had touched her.

"The Cavanaughs are incredibly tenacious, too, when it comes to staying in love," she told him. "After speaking to Melina on the phone, I made a tremendous effort to get over you and fall for another man. As long as I kept my eyes open I could almost convince myself that I liked him well enough to make it work. But when I closed them and started listening to my heart, I knew there was only one person in the world for me."

Wrapped in each other's arms, they moved away from the parquet entryway, along the whispery hall runner and onto the plush bedroom carpet. Casi breathed deeply of that intimate atmosphere and gloried in the strong, secure nearness of Nicholas as he lifted her in his arms to lay her across the bed.

She was alive again, Casi thought exultantly, reveling in the excitement of all her senses. Until that last evening with Wayne, she had almost forgotten the promise she had made to herself, the vow to experience life with every priceless gift at her command.

Vision, a fabulous new dimension, had now been added to her relationship with Nicholas. But never again would she allow any of that other, variegated enjoyment to slip by her without being fully utilized.

He pulled off her shoes and slid the jacket away from her shoulders. "It's Saturday," he said. "About thirty weeks late, but it's Saturday. Does that remind you of anything?"

A happy glow of reminiscence spread across Casi's face. "The first time we made love you promised to ask me again to marry you—on Saturday. And if I said no you threatened to kidnap me."

"Got it backward, didn't I?" A devilish grin flashed across his face, sparkling his eyes, as he recalled that the kidnapping had already taken place. But when he took in the joy of her expression the grin faded, to be replaced by a look of tender affection.

"Will you, sweetheart? Marry me, please?"

"Oh, Nicholas, yes!" Casi sighed ardently. "Yes! As soon as we can round up the witnesses or have the banns called out. I don't care where or when or how, as long as we can stay together always. Now that I have you back, I don't ever want to be without you again."

He gazed down at the woman who was infinitely dear to him. "Casi, darling, make love to me with your eyes."

She held out her arms to him. "For the rest of my life I intend to love you with my eyes. And my ears and nose and fingers. . . ."

And always, always, Casi thought, she would listen to that inner rhapsody—the sweet, lilting music that came from sharing her life with Nicholas.

Harlequin Temptation

COMING NEXT MONTH

#93 SLOW MELT Jane Silverwood

The moment Kate met Chris in a change room, she realized he was exceptional. Even with his clothes *on*, she wanted to see more and more of him....

#94 A WEEK FROM FRIDAY
Georgia Bockoven

Repossessing a man's car was one way to earn money—and guaranteed to disenchant the owner. Yet when Eric caught Janet in the act, he was anything but turned off....

#95 STAR-CROSSED Regan Forest

Living together for fourteen days in the wild made them friends. Sharing fourteen nights under a canopy of stars made them lovers. But sharing a lifetime seemed no more than a dream....

#96 WITHOUT PRECEDENT JoAnn Ross

Jessica was a divorce lawyer, and highly skeptical about happy ever afters. Which was just what Quinn had in mind for them....

Take
4 novels
and a
surprise gift
FREE

Harlequin Intrigue

Because romance can be quite an adventure.

1